UnWritten

UnWritten is a fine piece of storytelling. I was captured from the first paragraph and was never disappointed as I ripped through each story, each life, and each new nugget of gold mined from the deepest truths and emotions of the human heart. This collection of characters and their respective "stories" are bound together by the ongoing drama of Raphael, a lovable heavenly messenger. H. E. Hobson is skilled at peeling back the veneer of "life" to expose what are the truest treasures in this earthly journey. I highly recommend *UnWritten* to all who love a good story, which causes you to take stock in your essential relationships!

Tommy D. York
College & Career Pastor

I was deeply moved from the first moment I picked up this book. This story has a way of opening up parts of your heart that may have been dormant or hiding. I believe all those who read this will be encouraged and challenged to live without regrets for the glory of God. As I know the author personally, his life bears the same mark on people, and I'm glad he wrote this.

Derek Joseph Levendusky
Speaker, Author, Musician

Hobson's book reminds us all that we are not alone in this world and there is more to life than we can see. Read *UnWritten* and be challenged to live a life without regrets.

Rick A. Mills
Author, Speaker, and America's Youth Pastor Coach

UnWritten is brilliant, refreshing and a beautiful reminder that God truly works in mysterious ways. It is a powerful story with clever and surprising characters that jump off the page. Hobson's perfect blend of humor, love, and redemption makes *UnWritten* an instant classic.

Alissa K. Whyman
Mother, Child Care Specialist

UnWritten

By H. E. Hobson

UnWritten
ISBN: 978-0-88144-121-5

Published by
Yorkshire Publishing
9731 East 54th Street
Tulsa, OK 74146
www.yorkshirepublishing.com

DEDICATED TO

Linda Kay Smith

Thank you
for teaching us how to live.

CHAPTER 1

Two tons of skidding metal screeched to a halt as an innocent bystander leapt to safety. The two paramedics in the ambulance—Marco and Blaine—were relieved.

No need to make this any worse, Blaine thought.

The paramedics threw open their doors and leapt from their seats. The man they almost hit yelled obscenities and waved his arms. An apology was in order, but a nod and a "sorry" was all they had time for. They saw the mangled body lying in a mixture of dust, weeds, and discarded debris. Blaine, having been a paramedic for fifteen years, could not disguise his helpless stare as Marco looked to him for some sense of hope.

"C'mon partner, let's save a life!" Blaine said. His words did not match his expression and tone.

Blaine and Marco were professionals; saving lives is what they did and most days they loved their jobs. However, this would not be one of those days. The report they would soon fill out would state they did everything they could. In the end, their best efforts would not be enough.

As Blaine performed CPR on the young woman, Marco caught sight of her wallet. It had flown out of her purse, which was a few feet away stuck in a puddle of mud. He looked for ID as he rummaged through her credit cards. Her license revealed her name was Lucinda Lincoln.

"Twenty six, and oh...she just had a birthday!" Marco said as he shook his head.

His facial expression revealed what he was thinking. *Too young to die,* he thought, *too young to die.*

Unbeknownst to the two paramedics, another being was methodically drifting toward the now crowded scene. Onlookers pushed as close as they could without crossing the established police barricade. The unseen figure slipped through the sea of people and past the police line. He was always amazed at how the most destructive events seemed to bring out the largest crowds. Invisible, he leaned down beside the frustrated paramedics and put his hand on the forehead of Lucinda Lincoln. The throng of spectators continued to watch a lifeless body as he observed Lucinda open her eyes. She sprung up from the ground and frantically began to scurry through the crowd. He knew what she was thinking; he saw this reaction all the time.

Lucinda froze in stunned bewilderment as she observed what appeared to be herself lying on the side of the road. The body was barely recognizable, but she knew it was her. As she approached the being lingering beside her body, a strange light emitted from all around him—otherwise, he looked like any other face in the crowd. The manner in which he turned to meet her let her know he was waiting for her.

She screamed, "Who are you? What's happening?" Then, before he could respond, she cried out, "Am I…dead?"

This is where Raphael's job became interesting. No matter how many times he watched people face the reality of their own death, it never seemed to prepare him for the next encounter. How did he answer such questions? Lucinda was, in human terms, dead. However, how did Raphael explain who he was and why he was there? He was an angel, but his assignment was "classified"; his commission came straight from the Commander.

Raphael was technically an interviewer, sent down to interrupt selected individuals who were passing on from this life into their eternal destination. Some were going up; some were going down. The Commander wanted Raphael to listen to the hearts of the individuals and document their feelings, thoughts, and any desires they had not found the time to express to the people around them. Raphael collected and delivered "The UnWritten Letters."

Lucinda looked into the eyes of Raphael and asked again, "Who are you?"

"Well, let's just say I am someone you need to talk to," replied Raphael.

"Am I dead?"

Raphael avoided the question, "The only thing I can tell is that you are being given an opportunity. You have a chance to communicate one more time before you leave."

Panic filled her voice as Lucinda screamed, "Before I leave? What? I don't understand! You mean I'm really dead! But how can that be? I need to do some things, like finish college; I would like to get married someday, maybe have some kids. Besides that, what about my family and friends? There are so many people I need to..."

Lucinda fell to the ground and sobbed uncontrollably.

Raphael waited a minute before answering. He tried to comfort her with a gentle touch on the cheek. She stopped crying and looked up at him.

"I know you have a lot of questions, and I wish I had some answers. But what if..." Raphael paused. Communicating this unusual opportunity was never easy.

He looked directly into her eyes, "What if you could communicate to whoever you wanted before you left this earth...what would you say to them?"

Lucinda looked at him and shook her head.

"Communicate? I don't want to communicate! I just want to stop being dead!" She stood up and looked around at the crowd of people. She saw the two paramedics still leaning over her body attempting to resuscitate her.

"That's me, isn't it?" she half remarked, half asked.

Raphael nodded his head. She already knew the truth.

Lucinda noticed how slowly everyone else was moving; they almost seemed frozen.

"Can they hear us?"

Again, Raphael shook his head, this time indicating "no."

"How much time do I have?" Lucinda asked.

"As much time as you need, but with a few conditions; I can only let one person know what you are about to share, and I can only communicate to them words that will bring healing, comfort, or love—Commander's orders."

"Commander? Do you mean God!"

Raphael nodded assuredly.

"Wow! God sent you to me? Then...you are an angel?"

"Yes," Raphael said with an uncomfortable smile, "But that is irrelevant, what is important is what do you need to say and who do you need to say it to."

"This is crazy!" Lucinda paced back and forth chewing on fingernails that did not exist.

Raphael just watched. He had learned to be patient in these moments.

Lucinda stopped. She opened her mouth and voiced one word, "Mom."

She paused and stared at absolutely nothing. A whisper revealed her thought, "If only I could speak to her one more time."

He had been waiting for this moment. Raphael moved toward Lucinda and placed his hand on her shoulder.

"Listen, as much as you would like to, it will be impossible for you to see her or talk to her directly. But, share with me what you need to say and I will make sure she gets the message."

"Well," Lucinda began, "Where do I start?"

"Start with your heart," Raphael said.

CHAPTER 2

Two weeks after Lucinda's death, her mother, Patrice, was finally going to clear out Lucinda's apartment.

After the memorial service, Patrice seldom left her house. She secluded herself behind the walls of her home, wallowing in a tear-filled sea of regret. She was numb, angry, sad, and, most of all, she was burdened with remorse. Over the last few years, her relationship with her daughter had not been good. Of course, she blamed herself and could not help but wonder if Lucinda's death was some kind of punishment from God. She put off going to Lucinda's apartment as long as she could. Just the thought of seeing anything that belonged to Lucinda brought a sense of gloom and despair.

Now, Patrice stood at the threshold of Lucinda's home. Trembling, she put the key in the lock and turned. She stepped inside. As she closed the door behind her, the tears began to stream down her face once again. Numb to their presence, she did not even wipe them away.

She plopped down on the couch and placed her face in the middle of a nearby pillow. She sobbed from the depth of her soul. It was a deafening, disturbing cry that she did not want the nearby neighbors to hear. The loss of her daughter was painful, although it was the remorse of how utterly dysfunctional their relationship had become that made the present pain unbearable. She could not remember the last time they experienced a cheerful moment together.

Patrice sat on the couch staring at everything around her. She was yearning for one more moment with her precious Lucinda. Yet, she was also unsure if she was ready to be here. Perhaps it was too soon to go through Lucinda's stuff. With that thought, Patrice stood up and turned to leave. In her fragile state of mind, she was not looking in front of her and ran right into the coffee table. As she slipped backwards, her hand caught the corner of the nearest couch cushion. The cushion flew up and landed on top of her as she crashed to the floor. The impact caused her to blank out for a moment. Her eyes opened to what appeared to be a spinning room. She grabbed the corner of the couch and pulled herself up. As she did, she saw it.

Sticking out of the side of the couch where the cushion had been was the corner of an envelope. She stumbled over to see what it was, rubbed the back of her head, and muttered something in Italian (the language she only used when angry, confused, or in the presence of other elderly Italian women). She pulled the envelope out of its secured place in the couch and turned it over. The word on the front of the envelope seemed to lift off the page as it seared into Patrice's eyes and right into her heart: MOM.

She stared at the envelope she was holding in her hand. She could not imagine what it contained. The thought of being able to read any words written by her daughter made her heart jump with a strange expectation.

Then, a surge of altered concern overwhelmed her. She flung the letter down on the table as her expression revealed the mix of fear, remorse, and utter disbelief coursing through her mind. Her last conversation with Lucinda contained a lot of anger and rage—on both of their parts. She wondered if the letter was just a continuation of that argument.

Patrice sat down on the couch and contemplated what to do next. She longed to experience anything that came from Lucinda, but was afraid of what that might be.

She sat back on the couch, took a deep breath, and closed her eyes. A few seconds later, she opened them and tore into the envelope like a five-year old at Christmas. She pulled the letter from the envelope, unfolded it, and began to read. Her eyes twinkled even as she continued to cry.

Mom,

I don't know quite how to start so I will begin with this: Mom...I love you. Through all of the misunderstandings and intense disagreements, I always loved you. I just wish I had taken the time to tell you, but unfortunately, I was so busy judging you and being critical of you, that there was no time to say what needed to be said and do what needed to be done. Do...I don't really know what I was supposed to do in our relationship, but as I think about it, maybe that's not what relationships are about...doing. Maybe relationships are really more about being. Being who you are and allowing others to be who they are. I wish I had just appreciated you for who you were. I wish I had just loved you unconditionally without judging every little thing you said and did.

I know that the last few years we both have said a lot of things that we really didn't mean and that we both regret. You think that you have your whole life in front of you to make things right. But, the truth is...we only have today to treat people with love and to tell them how much we appreciate them. Of course, now, I don't even have that.

However, somehow in a way that I do not understand, I received this chance to say what I had neglected to say before. And now as I try to communicate from my heart all that I want to tell you, I realize that my words fall short. So, I thought I would leave you with a memory.

I was just thinking about that one day in June right after I had graduated from high school. It was a Saturday and Dad was away on business and you called me to see if I wanted to go shopping. Do you remember? Mom, it was probably the best day of my life. You and I spent the whole day with no schedule, no stress, no plan; it was so amazing. I can remember when we ordered ice cream cones, and as soon as you paid for them, you turned around and ran right into that enormous man! Remember? Your ice cream went all over his shirt and then you slipped and fell right into the middle of his belly and your face was covered with fudge ripple and broken pieces of cone! That man looked at you and began to yell as loud as he could, calling you every name in the book. I was so scared! But then, right in the middle of that man's tirade, you and I looked and caught each other's eye and, at the exact same moment, we both burst out laughing! I spewed the ice cream that was in my mouth all over the man who was now turning red with anger and yelling even louder. We ran out of that little ice cream shop and across the mall... both of us in high heels, purses flying up in the air and laughing at the top of our lungs! I remember we ran clear to the other side of the mall and took the elevator to the top level. We wanted to make sure that we didn't run into "The Giant." To make sure we didn't see him again we went into the movie theater and when the girl at the counter asked what we wanted to see, we just frantically said, "Whatever is showing next." The girl got that perplexed look on her face and asked, "Are you sure?" You just threw her the money, grabbed the tickets, and we both ran to theatre number three, never looking to see what movie we were going into. Do you remember what we saw that day? I do...we just so happened to go into an all-day showing of the Disney Princess movies. Who ever heard of such a thing—A Princess Movies Marathon! Strange! At first, we were not going to stay. You and I had always been more into "grown up" girl movies—chick flicks. In fact, I do not remember ever watching one of the little girl "Princess" movies. But then we ended up watching, Cinderella, Snow White, and Sleeping Beauty, and I loved them. I think you did too. The entire time we were in there you still had the ice cream and cone all over the front of you, and for some reason, neither one of us even cared. I remember that we kept looking over our shoulders to see if the Big Man was coming into the theater! Why we thought that he would come into the "all-day" princess marathon was hilarious.

I remember when we finally got up the nerve to leave the theater; we went and bought you a new top, so of course you had to have a purse and shoes to match. You looked so good in your new attire that we decided I had to have a new outfit also. If I remember correctly, we used Dad's "emergency only" credit card! I still don't know how you explained that to him. To top off the evening we decided to show off our wonderful new outfits at the "Evening Glade"—the nicest restaurant in town. You told me I could order anything I wanted, and we laughed aloud again as you held up Dad's emergency credit card for one more bail out! I remember that I ordered the steak and lobster. If you remember correctly, that was my first and last lobster. Still don't see what all of the fuss is about.

After we left the restaurant, we went back to the house and just sat in the porch swing talking all night long. I remember waking up with my head in your lap.

Mom...That was the best day of my life! We weren't trying to fix each other or make everything better. We just enjoyed being together and it seemed like every moment of that day was filled with joy.

I beg of you to remember that day. I am asking you with everything in my heart—please do not live with any regrets concerning me. Just remember that day when we loved each other and accepted each other without question.

One last thing...

I want you to know that I know.

I know that you loved me. I know that you always wanted the best for me. I know that you truly cared. I know you sacrificed for me. I know that you did your best.

I never said it enough, but you were a wonderful mother.

I love you, mom, and I hope to see you again.

Lucinda

Raphael smiled as he watched Patrice read the letter repeatedly. He knew the days ahead would be difficult for her, but, at least now, Patrice had something that was truly from her daughter's heart.

Raphael ducked into the hallway and pulled out what looked like a clear spiral notebook. He glanced down and pressed an invisible button. A list of names appeared. He quickly looked over the list making sure to check the times recorded by each name. He almost let out a shout when he realized his next assignment was over five hundred miles away. Not too far to fly by angel standards, but still, he would need to hurry. Raphael took one last look at Patrice as he silently flew out of the room.

CHAPTER 3

Beth cried as the hand she had been holding for the last two days went limp. The blank look in her eyes revealed the weariness of body and soul that only comes when all hope is lost. Doctors and nurses frantically pushed past her. The unrelenting tone of the heart monitor signaled the loss of life and pierced through all of the commotion: Beth heard nothing else. She stumbled backwards in a sleep-deprived daze. She did not even notice when her father wrapped his arms around her and saved her from running into the small table shoved against the hospital wall.

Is the room spinning? Am I falling? Who are all of these people? Her thoughts mingled into a toxic concoction of confused sentiment.

She felt herself shut down. With no strength left in her body, she closed her eyes and allowed herself to go limp. She fell into her father's embrace with the loud cry of her mother's voice being the last thing she heard, then... nothing.

Beth opened her eyes. Startled by the darkness that appeared to have severed her ability to see, she struggled to fight her way out of an overly tightened bed sheet.

Beth said aloud, "My God...why is it my mom doesn't think a bed is properly made unless it's a struggle to get in and out of?"

The sun light struck her face as she disposed of her momentary "blindness" by crawling out from under the bed covers. The darkness was gone, but the emptiness in her soul lingered. She looked at the clock and realized almost an entire day had gone by since she had let go of Andi's hand.

"Oh man, do I need to pee!" Beth whispered to herself.

As she made her way across her room, she heard the sound of footsteps scampering up the stairs. She stepped back knowing her mom was about to explode through the doorway in an emotional outburst. Beth braced herself.

"Beth... are you up?"

The door flew open and her mom pounced into the room. She gave Beth a simultaneous hug and kiss. This became an awkward embrace as her mother refused to let go and began her infamous habit of speaking without taking a breath.

"Oh Beth, I love you! Are you Ok? I know this is hard. We all miss him! You meant so much to our little Andi. I know he loved you. There was nothing we could do. I am sure he is in a better place; don't you think so? He's really better off, not that I want him to be gone, oh don't misunderstand me Beth... we all loved him. Everyone is so worried about you, are you ok? You just collapsed into your daddy's arms; we didn't know what was wrong. I told everyone you were okay... you are okay aren't you? You slept for so long, but I kept checking on you every hour or so; your dad said it was just good for you to sleep... I don't think you slept the whole time you were with little Andi. I'm sure he knew you were there… don't you think, or maybe he didn't know anything, I never knew what Andi was thinking or if he was thinking… well surely he had thoughts… don't you think? Oh Beth, I love you so much… now get dressed and come downstairs, I made you breakfast… though it's almost lunch time, but I'll warm it up for you, unless you want something else…well, just come down and I'll make you something to eat."

With that, her mom let Beth go and nervously scurried out of the room.

"John! Beth is up and she's coming down to get something to eat." She turned and poked her head back in Beth's room for one more clarification, "Come right down, Beth, everyone's been worried and your father would really like to see you."

It's a wonder my mom hasn't had a heart attack or developed an ulcer, Beth thought.

Still having to use the bathroom, she promptly made her way out of the bedroom and down the hall. The emotional numbness she woke up to subsided as her eyes caught a glimpse of her brother Andi's picture hanging by the mirror. She shut the bathroom door so no one could see her tears or hear her cries.

Andi observed Beth collapse into the arms of his father; he listened to his mother's cries of anguish. He noticed all the doctors and nurses bustling around the bed.

"I was just in that bed," he thought, "This is strange."

"If you think that is strange, well...it is about to get a whole lot stranger," Raphael calmly stated.

Andi screamed, "AAAWWWWWWWW! Who are you?"

Andi fell back in shock at the sound of his own voice. This was the first time he had ever heard it. In fact, Andi had never spoken, walked, or voluntarily moved in any way. For twenty-one years, he had only existed.

Raphael approached to help him up and said with a smile, "How you doing, Andi?"

Andi cautiously allowed Raphael to help him up and then shouted, "Can you hear me?"

"Of course."

"How is it that you can hear me, and how is it that I'm standing and walking and talking? No one has ever heard me talk!"

"Well..." Raphael began to say.

Before he could continue, Andi pointed at his sister Beth laying in their father's arms and blurted, "Is she Ok?"

"Yes she's fine..." Raphael began again.

Then Andi saw what appeared to be himself laying under the team of frenzied doctors and nurses and exclaimed, "Oh my God... is that me! Awwww...What is happening! Suddenly I can walk, I can talk, and no one knows I am here, do they? Is this a dream? Why can't they see me? What is this?"

Raphael attempted to calm Andi down, however Andi was already across the room looking up into his father's face. "Dad...it's me...Andi! I'm here and I can talk! Look at me, Dad! I can walk and talk."

Andi was jumping up and down in front of his dad and yelling as loud as he could, "Daaaaaad! I am here!" He attempted to punch his dad, but his hand seemed to go right through him. "I am here, Dad...I am right here. Please, Dad...please look at me...Please, Dad...talk to me." Andi's voice became more and more quiet with each plea as he slumped down at his father's feet. "Oh Dad, I just want you to hear me just once."

Raphael slowly made his way across the room. He gently put his hand on Andi's shoulder.

He responded by looking up at Raphael and exclaiming, "If you're like the death angel or something, you just need to know that I'm going up." He continued very matter-of-factly, "Beth told me what I needed to do to go to heaven and I did it, so if I'm dead you better take me to the right place!"

Raphael quietly chuckled then said, "Alright, Andi. I'll let you discuss that with the Commander, you will see Him later. That's not why I'm here."

"Then I'm not dead?"

"No, you are what you would call dead; I am just not here to take you somewhere...I have a different job."

Andi looked up at Raphael and slipped out a confused, "Huh?"

Raphael hated having to explain himself. Sometimes he just wanted to be a normal angel with a normal assignment. He often wondered what it would be like to be an "Eternity Escort." Many people called them "Death Angels," but his friends in that line of work preferred "Eternity Escort." Oh well, these thoughts were immaterial because he needed to take care of the business at hand.

This assignment provided Raphael with a strange mix of emotions. The death of Andi was tragic. Yet, it also afforded him the opportunity to share his heart, his thoughts, and his words for the very first time.

Andi possessed a rare disease Raphael could not even pronounce. All he knew was Andi had been mute and mostly paralyzed from birth. He could not even make a sound. He could sometimes move his arms, but the movements were always random and uncontrolled.

He could hear though. Unfortunately, this allowed him to hear many cruel comments from people. It had also allowed him to hear the frustration and sometimes uncompassionate words of his own family, especially his mom and dad. They always presumed that because Andi could not express his thoughts, he also could not understand. He wondered how things might have been if they had known how brilliantly smart he was and how he understood every word they ever spoke.

"If you're not here to take me somewhere, then…what are you here for? You are an angel, aren't you?" Andi posed the questions with both a puzzled stare and unsure tone. He still could not get used to the sound of his own voice.

Raphael explained to Andi who he was and what he did.

"Wow," Andi said, "Cool job!"

At this, Raphael smiled back. Andi was right. As much as Raphael struggled with what he did, it was definitely a unique line of work—even for an angel.

"So, Andi…You just need to share your heart. Say what you want to say to one person. I know that may be difficult, because you may want to talk to many people, but… I don't make the rules; one letter to one person." Raphael paused to give Andi a moment to think it over.

"So…who's it going to be?"

Andi was taking his time. His soul was flooded with a million thoughts and memories. This really was not a difficult decision for him. Even though they treated him like a child and often spoke words that deeply wounded him, he loved his parents. He knew they had done their best. He had many therapists, doctors, and nurses who showed great compassion and kindness toward him. Nevertheless, in Andi's mind, there was only one person who understood him and loved him…Beth. Beth was his older sister by three years and his only sibling. Andi often wondered if he was the reason Mom and Dad never had more children. He overheard them on a few occasions discussing the possibility. Then he would hear his name in the conversation and…no other children ever came.

"Beth," Andi whispered.

Raphael smiled with a gleam in his eye. *This is one letter I can't wait to deliver,* he thought.

Most of the letters he delivered were because people did not take the time to say what they needed to say while they were living. Andi was different. He never had the opportunity to express his love, his thoughts, and his feelings.

Raphael looked warmly at Andi, "Well…let's get started."

CHAPTER 4

Beth ran up the stairs and slammed the door to her room. Her mother was right behind her and knocked on the door almost as soon as it closed.

"Honey, are you all right?"

Beth attempted to ignore her mother, but she knew that would not work. "Mom, I'm fine! I just need some time to myself."

"Ok, dear. We'll all be downstairs. Take your time, but not too much time. It's not good to be alone right now."

They had just returned from Andi's memorial service. The service was beautiful and the crowd was larger than expected. Beth was astonished to see some of the people who were there. People who had mocked Andi and shunned Beth were there today crying and hugging Beth as if she was their best friend. Oh, how she hated hypocrisy.

The music was great, and Pastor Murdock preached a wonderful message with the perfect mix of compassion, sentiment, and conviction.

"Oh Andi, I wish you could have been there today. Everyone was talking about you! They even let me pick out the music. I just told them, 'Nothing sad...keep it upbeat!' They sure did that. You would have loved the choir today. They really put on a show for you!"

Beth wiped the tears cascading down her face. After the last four days, it was difficult to believe there were any tears left.

She endeavored to open her bedroom door and quietly slip out without her mother knowing. As she tiptoed down the hallway, she could hear her mother sputtering out one sentence after another which assured her she was in the clear. She quietly made her way down the hall to the last door on the left—Andi's room. She could remember all of the arguments that ensued when her mother insisted on Andi's room being on the second floor.

"It doesn't make sense," her dad had asserted.

In the end, the second floor won out. They made it work somehow. The local churches and several charities raised the funds for the installation of a special elevator in order for Andi to be transported back and forth between floors. The house was not that big, so the elevator was quite a site. People actually came over for a visit just in order to see it. Beth did not mind though, she always loved riding the elevator.

She entered Andi's room and closed the door behind her. She did not know why, but she always felt at peace in this room. No matter what she was going through, she could always go into Andi's room and find refuge. Sometimes she would talk to Andi, other times she would just lie on the floor. She used to crank up the stereo and dance around. She shared everything with Andi. She never had a diary, because she never needed one.

She began looking around the room, sifting through pictures and a stack of cards on the corner of the desk that were primarily from Andi's last birthday. As she was reading some of the cards, she noticed what looked like an unopened envelope sitting on the very back of the right side of the desk. She picked it up and turned it over...

Beth hoped her mom did not hear the thud as she collapsed to the floor. She was now sitting with her legs crossed holding a sealed envelope that read "To: Beth, From: Andi" in a handwriting she did not recognize.

Is this a cruel joke? Beth thought, *or is this my mother's lame attempt to console me?*

There was only one way to find out. Beth held her breath and ripped the corner from the envelope. She slowly pulled the letter from inside and unfolded the first page.

Beth,

Is this weird or what? I cannot believe this has happened. All my life I have been trapped in a body, in an existence that did not allow me to express myself. Now, I have the ability to say anything I want, but then I will be gone. Strange! I want to shout aloud... AAAAHHHHHHHHHHHH! I want to talk to everyone. I want to speak to the whole world, and believe me... I have a LOT to say! But I have been told I can only speak to one person. And that person is you.

Beth, you are the only one that ever understood me and loved me unconditionally. I know Mom and Dad meant well. But they always talked to me like I was two years old. I know I couldn't speak or express what I was thinking, but it didn't mean that I couldn't hear or understand! I was twenty-one years old and everybody still spoke to me like I was a little baby, everyone but you! You always treated me as if I was someone, like I wasn't handicapped, like I was your equal, like I was your best friend. It must have been hard when you were teased by your school friends because of me. I'm sorry for all that you went through. I knew what was going on. I heard the taunting of cruel neighborhood kids and the constant arguing from Mom and Dad about what to do with me; and yet, it never seemed to bother you. It was as if you knew I could understand what they were saying.

I remember when Mom and Dad would be arguing and Dad would yell about "The Big Dummy" (it really hurt me when he called me that); you would just turn up the music so that I would not hear. You protected me, and you gave up popularity for me, and even some friends and boyfriends for me... Why did you do that?

I so often observed people trying to figure out what love is, and I just wanted to yell at the top of my lungs, "Look at Beth! She's the only one that knows how to show love!" I remember hearing some person on the radio once, and he said something like, "No greater love has anyone than he that lays down his life for his friends." I couldn't show it, but when I heard that I wanted to smile and cry at the same time, because I knew that was what you were doing. You loved me!

Oh Beth, there are so many things I want to say, I could probably fill an entire book. Speaking of books, I want to thank you for reading aloud all the time so I could hear. You read so many books and you could have just read them to yourself. You didn't have to come in my room and read every one of them aloud. Because of you, I know the "classics"; I know history and even some trigonometry, though I don't know why you did your homework aloud, but...thanks! You even shared some romance novels—censored of course! I also loved when you read the Bible. You always made it come alive and seem so real.

Beth, you also talked to me about everything. I don't know if you realized I could understand you, but it just always meant so much to me that you included me in your life. I know all about your boyfriends—even the ones that didn't come back because of me—and which girls you were really friends with and which ones you were just nice to...I heard it all! There were a few times I wished that I could walk because I wanted to hit some of the stupid boys you dated. Oh, by the way...I saw your first kiss! Mom and dad were gone and you were supposed to be watching me. Then Reggie came over. Oh yeah...sorry! I know you thought I was asleep!

Beth, I know you are sad that I am gone, but now it is time for you to live your life. You are a loving, caring, beautiful person and I'm not quite sure how things work on my side, but if I have any say in what happens to you in your life, I am going to make sure that you have a great guy that will love you and treat you like you deserve. I am going to meet the Commander soon (I think that's God!), and I will try to put in a good word for you.

Don't cry for me, because now I can talk, and walk and dance and run, and shout, and make noise and jump and smile...

Beth, I will miss you, but I know I will see you again. You know how to get here and I heard you when you told me how...I was listening and I knew if you said it, it had to be true.

Please don't tell Mom or Dad what I said about them, I know they tried their best.

You are the most beautiful soul alive and the only one who always treated me as if I was a person. I love you and...

Goodbye

Andi

Raphael watched as Beth cried and laughed and cried again.

He reached up to his own face as he felt wetness gathering under his own eyes. *What am I doing?* Raphael thought. *Angels aren't supposed to cry!*

He quickly wiped his tears and looked around. He was invisible to Beth and there was no one else there; but he wanted to be certain. The "UnWritten Letter Project" was a classified mission. However, many angels knew about it. Somehow, the fact that his job was unusual made Raphael feel inferior at times. He wondered why the Commander chose him for this type of work and not a normal angelic duty, like guardian or messenger.

These thoughts went with him as he flew out the window to his next assignment.

CHAPTER 5

Ryan bolted down the alley with his gun firmly in his grip. His entire focus was on catching the would-be felon who disappeared into the maze of alleys, abandoned buildings, and unlit streets known as the Nance district. This section of town had once been the focal point of all pertinent business in the city. Now it was just a haven for pimps, prostitutes, drug lords, and thieves. Ryan and his fellow officers often noted, "The Nance district is so bad, even the gangs won't go there." And they were right. Gang leaders in this town all had their "turfs," but in the Nance, it was every man for himself.

The hoodlum on the run knocked over two drug stores and shot a clerk in the neck, all within twenty minutes. There was no word yet on the status of the clerk. Ryan and his partner, Lincoln, did not want this one to get away. The commissioner was under extreme pressure to crack down on the recent crime wave emitting from the Nance. The criminals were now beginning to infiltrate the "nicer" parts of the city. The Mayor was not pleased, especially since it was an election year. The pressure on the commissioner spilled down into the entire department. Everyone was feeling the squeeze. This was Ryan's opportunity to "step up to the plate" and "hit one out of the park" as the commissioner liked to say—repeatedly.

Ryan was now in the heart of the Nance. Here the shadows enveloped everything and everyone. He was running with his free hand out in front of him in case one of the shadows came to life. His heart was pounding as endless streams of sweat impaired his ability to see. He leaned against the corner of the old factory building at the end of the alley. He caught his breath and wiped his face and eyes. Even in his heightened sense of focus, his concentration was broken as he caught a whiff of himself.

Man do I stink!

Footsteps coming around the corner quickly interrupted this thought.

His partner Lincoln roared, "Stop... Stop or I'll shoot!"

"I've got him!" Ryan mumbled.

He tried to time the sound of the footsteps perfectly and then leapt from behind the corner and into the alley. His timing was too perfect and the owner of the footsteps was instantaneously in Ryan's face. He fell backward as the man plowed into him. Instinctively or accidently (an argument Ryan has yet to settle in his mind) Ryan fired his gun. The bullet burst into the man's chest and the man collapsed on top of him. Ryan propelled the man to the ground. In his adrenaline-induced state, he vaulted himself up and five feet away with his gun still drawn. His heart went beyond pounding and now resembled a bad drum line—eradicate and offbeat. His eyes were so wide open that blinking was impossible.

"I've got him!" Ryan yelled as Lincoln approached in the darkness.

Another figure ambled by just a few feet in front of him. Lincoln then appeared. He halted and looked at the man bleeding on the ground.

"Oh no, Ryan!" Lincoln said.

"What?" Ryan retorted.

Lincoln shook his head as he put his hand on Ryan's arm. "You shot the wrong guy!"

"Oh God, I thought...he ran into me...I...oh man, what have I done?"

"Call for an ambulance!" Lincoln barked as he disappeared in the darkness still in pursuit of the criminal.

Ryan grabbed his radio and called for help. He then knelt down in front of the man struggling for his life.

"Don't die," Ryan cried, "You can't die! Stay with me."

Blood was pouring out of the man's mouth, which made it impossible for Ryan to perform CPR. He continued to put pressure on the gunshot wound and try to stop some of the bleeding. Minutes seemed liked hours as he waited for help.

"Where is that ambulance?" Ryan screamed aloud. "What is taking them so long?"

Just then, Ryan heard the familiar sound of the rescue siren. He hoped there was still time.

"Hold on, buddy! Hold on!" Ryan stood up to signal his location to the paramedics. "We're over here!" he yelled.

As Ryan knelt down beside the man again, he heard a loud gurgle as blood spewed out of his mouth and chest.

"No!" He shrieked.

He fell back and a paramedic steadied him with his hand. Ryan stared at Marco and Blaine as they furiously labored to save the stranger's life. He had worked with these two before. He knew they were dedicated and would do their best.

In the shadow of the adjacent building, Raphael waited knowing that once again Marco and Blaine's best efforts would not be enough. Raphael could not help but feel sorry for the two of them. In addition, his heart broke for Ryan.

In these moments, he yearned for the ability to do more than just write letters. He envisioned himself appearing early and stopping this entire tragedy. It was a frequent vision, but never reality. He had friends who were "guardians," but not Raphael. He was not even a "messenger" angel. No, right now he just felt like a glorified secretary that took dictation.

Raphael pulled himself together as the man's heart completely stopped. Marco and Blaine put him in the ambulance and once again went through the motions of trying to save his life. Though Marco discouraged him, Ryan insisted on riding along.

Raphael just shook his head and got ready to meet Julio Levitz. He was already in the ambulance.

Appearing to Julio in the confines of a moving ambulance was not optimal. From Raphael's experience, people needed room to react when hearing the news of their own death. However, to Raphael's surprise, the initial response of Julio Levitz had not been as chaotic as he anticipated. In fact, he was unusually calm.

Raphael smiled as Julio stared at him in utter disbelief, "OK, so let me get this straight. That's me lying there and one more time you are...?"

"Who I am is really not important," Raphael calmly stated.

"Well, it's important to me!" Julio quipped. "I was jogging along in the dark, and the next thing I know, I wake up in this moving closet with you, my dead body, and a couple of guys who can't see me, one of which you say shot me!" Julio stared wide-eyed at Raphael as he hesitated for effect. "Listen...I most definitely want to know who you are, why you're here, and when I'm going to wake up from this messed up nightmare!"

Raphael hung his head and sighed. He realized why Julio was so calm. Julio did not think anything happening at the moment was real. This was not the first time Raphael had seen this happen. Consequently, he knew this would complicate the situation.

Raphael spoke, "This is not a dream. Everything I told you is true."

"You mean...this is real?" Julio said.

"Yes...this is real."

"You mean real, like I'm DEAD for real?" The words simultaneously came out as a question and an awakening statement.

Raphael now observed as the hysteria he foresaw erupted in the confined space of the ambulance. Fortunately, the only two who experienced the frenzied outburst were Raphael and Julio. Marco and Blaine were busy with the life-saving attempt while Officer Ryan mumbled a prayer and wrung his hands.

"I'm deee—aaaa—dddd!" Julio shouted as he unsuccessfully attempted to pull out the IV currently inserted in his dead body.

Raphael was somewhat accustomed to hysteria; with his current duties, emotional outbreaks were expected. However, he had never heard "dead" uttered as a multi-syllable word. That was new. Also, Raphael did not normally experience this kind of commotion in such a confined space. Julio was now attempting to jump out of the ambulance.

"Listen..." Raphael began.

"What? Mr. Death man? What!"

Death man...hmmm...that is also new, Raphael thought.

"What do you want with me? I am already dead! So what do you want? Can you change this? Huh? I don't think so! What is it you're here for again? You're here to make me feel better about being dead? Well if that's the case, you're not doing a very good job! Because I am not very happy!" Julio screamed out the words then collapsed to the one spot in the ambulance where there was a small section of open floor.

Raphael awaited this moment—the moment of breaking. Julio melted into a heap of human spirit and emotions. He cried long and hard, lifting his head up then throwing it down with each big sob. He went on like this for almost ten minutes: continuously sobbing without saying a word. His head was down and his tears were gone as the ambulance pulled into the hospital and Marco and Blaine wheeled Julio's body into the ER. Julio lifted his head and watched himself roll away.

"This is surreal...I am watching myself being pulled away on a death cart." Even as he said it, a strange calm overtook him. He was embracing the reality of the moment. Julio stepped out of the ambulance and Raphael carefully followed.

"So...whoever you are...why are you here again?" Julio questioned.

Once again, Raphael attempted to explain his purpose and the opportunity he was offering Julio. He had just come to the part about choosing one person with which to leave his final words.

Raphael thought about the many worthy choices Julio had. He had studied this case for quite a while and knew the family well. This family had already experienced tragedy, so any remaining family members would be a good choice for Julio. While meditating on this, Julio surprised him with this question.

"What about him? What's his name?"

Raphael turned to see at whom Julio was pointing. Ryan was sitting on the back of the open ambulance with a despondent expression: dazed eyes, quivering lip, and a pulsating blood vessel across the forehead. Julio was pointing right at him.

"Uh...well, that's Officer Ryan...the police officer who shot you."

"Accidentally shot me, right? I believe you told me this was an accident and he was just trying to do his job, correct?"

"Yes, that would be correct." Raphael held back from saying what he was thinking.

Rule number eight: Never influence someone's choice of whom they leave their final thoughts with.

For all angels there is a "Code of Conduct Manual." It contains general rules and guidelines concerning angelic behavior. However, since "The UnWritten Letter Project" was a special assignment, Raphael needed to follow a few additional rules he was given. He studied, memorized and knew them well.

Though he was not supposed to manipulate a person's choice, he generally knew whom they would select. Raphael thought this was a "no-brainer." Julio lost his sister in a drowning accident and his father to a heart attack. His mother and brother were both still alive and could probably use some words of encouragement.

The direction Julio appeared to be going was a surprise to Raphael.

"Do you know anything about him or his family? I mean, is he a good guy?" Julio asked.

"Well, I'm not really supposed to say anything that would influence your decision, but..." Raphael paused. He usually kept his opinions to himself. "...I just don't understand why you would not use this opportunity to encourage some of your own family members. This man is a total stranger and he..." Raphael stopped himself before he went any further. "Look, it is your choice."

"You bring up a good point, my family could use this, but you don't know my family. I truly believe they would want me to use this opportunity in this way. My people are going to need a lot of encouragement, I mean, we've faced some terrible tragedies already and now...this," Julio pointed at himself. "But my family has always taught me to think of others first and that if you give, others will give back to you. My mom and brother and even my grandpa are going to need more encouragement than I can give them. So I think I want to use this opportunity to encourage someone else and pray that others will do the same for my family."

Raphael had been at this point with many people; however, he had never heard anyone in this position be so selfless. He was astonished.

Julio continued as he gazed at Ryan, "This man is going to have a tough time with what he did...I can tell by looking at him." Julio continued to stare at Ryan as he voiced his final question to Raphael, "So, how do I do this?"

CHAPTER 6

Ryan had not slept and it showed. He held his head in his hands as he contemplated the consequences of running away. He would not run, but right now, it was a comforting alternative to his current nightmare.

How am I going to tell my wife? What is my son going to think of me when he grows up and learns of what I did? What am I going to say to this man's family? I just want to die!

The life of Julio Levitz officially terminated at 11:13 p.m. Ryan was now sitting in his office staring at a police report. He had been attempting to fill it out for the last two hours. He looked up at the clock; it was 3:35 a.m. He had another officer call his wife at midnight and let her know he would not be home and not to worry. If he knew his wife, she was in bed tossing and turning, waking up about every thirty minutes. Telling his wife not to worry was like telling a politician to be quiet; she was worrying.

At this time of night, the precinct offices were like a ghost town: the officers on duty were all on patrol. Ryan stood up and walked to his office window. He looked out at the empty desks and scattered dim lights that were still on.

"Knock, Knock."

The knock on the door startled Ryan.

"Where did that come from?" he mumbled.

He looked out and saw no one.

"Knock, Knock."

Again, the knock on the door bewildered him.

"Who is it?" Ryan said.

"Special delivery," a voice grunted from the other side of the door.

Raphael, completely visible, was dressed in a uniform doing his best to impersonate a human deliveryman while hiding behind the door. On the other side, Ryan was now wide-awake and wondered why a special deliveryman was making a delivery at 3:40 a.m. All of his training caused him to be suspicious.

Ryan took his gun from his holster. He pointed it at the door, hesitating as he thought about what he was doing.

"Who are you? Really?"

Again Raphael tried to disguise his voice, "Special delivery, I have something for you."

Immediately Ryan began to think, *Oh my God…someone has come here to kill me. Maybe it's someone from Julio's family!*

Raphael, concerned about Ryan, wanted to deliver Julio's letter to him as soon as possible and make sure he read it immediately. He planned to sneak into the office when Ryan went home, but he never went home. Thus, Raphael devised a plan to impersonate a deliveryman and give the letter right to Ryan. At present, Raphael wondered why he was doing this; he did not think Ryan was buying his act.

Most angels have the ability to be visible or invisible. In general, an angel is invisible to the living unless visibility is required for their particular job description. On a rare occasion, an angel will appear visible unintentionally if they are in a traumatic situation. Raphael, up to this point, had never appeared to the living. Occasionally, he would become visible when he was alone just to see if he could do it. However, this was the first time he intentionally used his visibility to impersonate a person. There was no rule that told him he could not, but he still worried about the whole deception thing.

"Listen," Raphael grunted again, "I am going to place a letter on the table and leave."

"Ok!" Ryan responded. He looked out and saw the arm of a deliveryman placing an envelope on an empty desk.

His instincts were still stirring. *Something is not right.*

"Hey," Ryan said, "Let me come out and talk to you."

No response.

"I just want to see your employee badge, OK? I am coming out."

Ryan looked out the window again. There was no way that the supposed deliveryman could have left that quickly. Besides, Ryan had not even heard the front door close.

Ryan opened the door then placed his hand on his re-holstered gun. He carefully scanned the entire office area. Nothing. Way on the other side of the office, he saw Officer Guild typing a report. Ryan walked over to Officer Guild's desk.

"Did you see anyone come in here?" Ryan asked.

Officer Guild turned and responded with an extremely annoyed tone, "What?" He saw it was Officer Ryan. "Oh, hey there. I didn't know you were still here. Uh...sorry to hear about, well... you know... I'm just sorry. You're in a lot of trouble, huh? What did you want?"

Ryan shook his head, "Nothing, go back to work...I was just getting some coffee."

He did not want to talk to anyone about the events of the day especially Officer Guild. It was not that they did not like each other; it was just that Officer Guild was very abrasive and annoying. Most of the other officers in the precinct avoided him.

It was this fact that troubled Ryan, *if he knows, then everyone knows.*

"I wouldn't drink the coffee...Gertrude made it, so you know it's bad—tastes like colored water, plus I think she made it two days ago. Sorry," Officer Guild said as he returned to his work.

Ryan turned to go back in his office then remembered he was looking for a "delivery guy" or an assassin. Raphael had already disappeared. He was too nervous to keep up his charade any longer. However, he did not leave. He was in a dark corner watching to make sure Ryan found the letter.

Ryan shook his head and wondered if he had dreamed the whole thing. Then he spotted it. The letter did not look like any delivery service letter he had ever seen. It was a plain white envelope with the words "Officer Ryan" written in fairly nice handwriting.

Anthrax? Ryan pondered.

He looked the envelope over repeatedly as he reentered his office and sat down at his desk.

So what if it is poisoned? Don't I deserve to die?

With this thought, Ryan pulled his letter opener from the top right-hand desk drawer. He opened the envelope and removed the letter. Raphael moved closer to get a good look at the stunned stare on Ryan's face.

Officer Ryan,

This may be the most bizarre thing that you have ever encountered and might be impossible for you to believe. I am having a difficult time with it myself. However, this is real. I am Julio Levitz, the one that you shot, and yes, these really are my words. I won't go into detail of how this is taking place, because you probably would not believe me anyway; but just know...this is really happening.

I was given the opportunity to communicate with one person before I go on to...well, before I go on, I think you know what I mean. Officer Ryan, I chose to communicate with you. Yes, I will be leaving behind family members and friends, and yes, there are many things that I would like to say to them. But, with one last chance to make my life count, I knew that communicating with you would be the greatest opportunity to make an impact. That is why it is so important that you listen to what I have to say as if your life depends upon it, because I believe it does. But not only does your life count on this...so does mine. That may sound strange, because my life is over, but listen to what I have to say and I think you will understand.

Because of what happened today, you are at a crucial point of decision. There may be consequences that come that are out of your control. However, your response to what happened is all up to you and will affect the lives of many, especially your wife and son. This moment in your life could be the beginning point of great tragedy that births a legacy of bitterness, anger, and self-loathing. Or, it could be the birthing of a legacy of forgiveness, kindness, and compassion that has the potential to flow out of your life and be something that is handed down from generation to generation. It is my desire to help you begin that legacy today. I want to begin the process by sincerely saying...I forgive you! And I want to continue by saying...I forgive you, I forgive you, I forgive you, I forgive you!

Raphael watched as Officer Ryan lay down the letter and began to weep. He shook uncontrollably. His tears were flowing from a deep place. Raphael had seen tears like this before. These are the kind of tears that lead to dead ends or new beginnings, soul cleansing or eternally bitter hearts. Officer Ryan attempted to wipe his tears, but the dam had broken and the flood had begun. He picked up the letter and began to read again.

I forgive you. My family will mourn my loss, but believe me...I know them, they will forgive you too. Our family has experienced a lot of tragedy, but we have learned that one tragedy is not healed by creating another. Your life needs not be a tragedy. You may be wondering how I can forgive you after what has taken place. I want to say...how can I not forgive you. You have and will pay a great price for your mistake; but how could my holding that against you at this moment change what has happened?

Right now, the only way my life will continue to matter will be if yours does. I don't want to sound selfish, but I need you to be strong as you walk out the days ahead. I need you to love your wife. I need you to raise your son. Ryan... I need you to forgive yourself. What you have done can never be changed, but it does not have to change you for the worse. It can change you for the better. Allow what has happened to cause you to appreciate everything you have been blessed with in a greater way. Appreciate your wife and son. Appreciate your job. Appreciate your life and the One who gave it to you. Appreciate every opportunity you have to breathe another breath, live another day, touch another soul. My plea to you is to never take what you have been blessed with for granted.

I will say it again, the greatest thing I am asking you to do is to forgive yourself. If you don't, then you will become bitter, angry and suspicious of everyone. Then your son will become the same. My life is over, but if my words to you today can cause you to embrace a path of forgiveness and change, then my life will continue to count. If you cannot forgive yourself for you, then do it for me...do it for your wife, do it for your son.

Ryan, your entire world is about to change, as is mine: not that we can compare the two. My eternal destiny is set, that happened while I was alive. However, your destiny is yet to be written. Do not let the memory of what happened with me destroy your future and the future of your family and everyone you meet. What you did was a mistake. A mistake made by a man just doing his job. Face whatever punishment you receive with courage. I can already see that you are a man that is broken and repentant over what you did. I saw you after it happened. I watched you in the ambulance and in the hospital parking lot. I know your heart is full of sorrow. You are not a man running from responsibility; you are a man afraid to forgive himself. Something inside you says that if you forgive yourself then that would somehow diminish the seriousness of what you did and take away from the preciousness of my life. I am telling you that the only way you can diminish my life is to destroy your own. You will make my life precious by embracing what I held dear. You will keep my memory alive by forgiving yourself and living a life worthy of following for the rest of your days.

Ryan, I know that it will be difficult to face my family. Nevertheless, please, when you see them, do not run away in shame, run to them in humility and brokenness. I know them...they will forgive you. Please understand, the reason my family and I can forgive you is our faith. We believe in a God who forgives, and believe me, I have needed a lot of forgiving.

Also, Ryan... do not run from your wife if she struggles with this and be honest with your son when he is old enough to understand. Your wife will appreciate you more when she sees your genuine brokenness and repentant heart. She may love you now, but she will love you more as she watches you take responsibility and face this trial like a man. Your son will forever look up to you because of your honesty and transparency. You will show him how to be a real man.

Ryan, I do not have anything else to say except to state one more time: I forgive you and my family forgives you, now please...forgive yourself. It is the greatest thing you can do for everyone.

Hoping to see you on the other side,

Julio

CHAPTER 7

Raphael was curious as to why the Commander would send him to acquire a letter from Mrs. Francis Buckley. *What could this woman possibly have left unsaid?* He thought. *She gave of herself her entire life and was not afraid to speak her mind.*

Normally, Raphael studied the file on the chosen person only once or twice before he met with them. Occasionally, though, he would do a little more research. After his initial study on Mrs. Buckley, he could not help but want to know more. She was an incredibly interesting person.

As an angel, Raphael had access to an unfathomable amount of information. However, he did not have unlimited access. There were some files only the Commander could view. In addition, when a person came to know the Commander, portions of their stored information mysteriously disappeared—as if the events never happened.

In researching, sometimes Raphael enjoyed a human perspective on someone else's life. Thus, he would enter a computer store after hours and Google the individual. There were over thirty thousand hits on Mrs. Francis Buckley. Apparently, she came from humble beginnings. However, she and her husband became quite wealthy when they discovered their modest little farm was sitting on one of the largest oil reserves ever discovered in the continental United States. They went from abject poverty to being multi-millionaires overnight. Mrs. Buckley's newfound wealth never seemed to change who she was. She and her husband were wise with their money, but she was also extremely generous. She used her wealth to help people in every way imaginable. Multiple homes for unwed mothers had her name on them, and several homeless shelters existed because of her generosity. She anonymously funded food programs in the United States and overseas, as well as establishing much needed water wells throughout the African continent.

Francis learned how to communicate in a way that caused other philanthropists to line up in hopes of being a part of her multiple ventures of compassion. She was a strong woman who spoke her mind but somehow did it in a way that inspired those around her. As she grew older, she became more and more vocal with her opinions. However, her strong communication was always in defense of her latest project or endeavors to help others.

Quite possibly Raphael was collecting a letter from Francis not because of what she left unsaid, but because of what needed to be read. Obviously, someone needed a reminder of the lessons that Francis had always provided for the pupil who was astute enough to listen.

"Now just who are you?" Francis asked Raphael.

"Well, I've been sent here for ..."

"Oh, I know why you're here." Francis interrupted, "I just wondered why He sent...you!"

"Excuse me?"

"Oh, you're excused...like I said; I was just expecting someone with a little more..." Francis looked Raphael up and down with her hand extended pointing in line with her gaze, "Well...someone with a little more something!"

"I'm sorry to disappoint, but maybe you don't realize why I am here."

"Oh, I told you, I know why you are here...I am dead, passed in my sleep. And I am excited about it!" Francis smiled as she shouted, "I am just disappointed that as good a friends as me and your Boss are...uh...you do work for the 'Man upstairs,' don't you?"

Before Raphael could speak, Francis answered her own question, "Well of course you do...I know where I am going. I just thought that He would send someone like Gabriel or something. No offense."

Wow...Raphael was speechless. Mrs. Francis Buckley was one spirited woman. He had anticipated meeting her, and now he just felt offended and wanted to leave.

Francis perceived Raphael's inner struggle and spoke again, "Now on the other hand, I must be quite special for Him..." Francis pointed up to clarify once again whom she was speaking of, "...to send you! Right?"

Raphael did not buy Mrs. Buckley's attempt at sincerity, but he did appreciate her effort to make him feel better.

"Listen, Mrs. Buckley..."

"Please, call me Francis." She said with a smile.

"OK, Francis. I just want to explain why I'm here."

"You mean you're not here to escort me to my 'Next Destination'?"

"No…I am not."

"Hotdog!" Francis excitedly exclaimed. "I knew it!" He's sending ol' Gabe, isn't He? Oh yeah…sending down one of His top angels to get the old broad! I knew it…I just knew it! Oh, me and Him have such a good relationship…I knew He would take care of me…I mean, He always has!"

Raphael was a bit surprised at how cavalier Mrs. Buckley seemed; not at all what he expected.

She may be generous, but this woman's crazy! he thought.

Then, without realizing it, he laughed aloud.

"Now what are you laughing at?"

"Oh, I'm sorry, was I laughing?" Raphael was embarrassed that he allowed his inner emotions to come out: very unprofessional.

"Don't be sorry because you laughed…uh…so what do they call you?"

"Well, I generally do not give out my name. I'm really not supposed to, just one of the rules of conduct."

"Rules of conduct?" Francis chuckled, "Now c'mon…what's your name?"

"Well…"

"Oh c'mon boy…tell this old lady your name…you're not going to get in trouble!"

"Ok..." Raphael looked around to see if anyone was watching or listening, "It's Raphael," he said with a slight smile.

"Well...that's a fine name, Raphael." Francis smiled. She looked deep into his eyes as if she were studying the deepest part of his angelic being. "Ok then, now why don't you tell me why you're here?"

Raphael explained his purpose for being there. Mrs. Buckley appeared genuinely interested in his every word. She asked a ton of clarifying questions and wanted to know more about him. They ended up talking for over two hours. Raphael began to understand why this woman had been so influential. It was not just her money; it was her demeanor. Sure, she came on strong at first, but he understood now it was because she was passionate about everything she did. He could tell that she was good friends with the Commander. There was always a certain glow about those who truly knew Him. Mrs. Buckley definitely knew Him, it poured out in her words, concern and the way she looked you in the eye.

Raphael wanted to keep talking with her, but he knew that he had to get on with his purpose for being there: Mrs. Buckley still needed to leave her unwritten letter.

He reminded her once again of why he was there, and she immediately said, "I know just who to leave my letter with!" As she spoke, her eyes twinkled and her mouth broke out in a smile. "Alright then, Raphael, let's get started."

CHAPTER 8

Funerals are so stupid! Maria thought.

She had just returned with her mother from the "Memorial Service." Now all she wanted was to go to her room. There were friends and family at the house, but she did not want to talk to anyone about anything; she especially did not want to discuss her grandmother.

Why do all of those people suddenly act like they care? she pondered. *I sure never saw them around when my Grandma was here. They're probably just hoping to get some of her money!*

Maria began to think of how nice everyone tried to be to her at the service. Many wealthy, influential people attended. She wondered if any of those people would have even talked to her if her grandmother had not died.

Some were ruthless business moguls who were not very nice. Her grandmother had influenced folks from every walk of life, and she was the same person to everyone she met: politicians, business people, clergy, white and blue-collar workers, and the homeless. To her, they were all the same.

"Those people didn't deserve to even know my grandma!" she angrily seethed through her teeth. "Why God... Why!" Maria looked up as she questioned aloud, "Why my grandmother? Why not some of them low-life scum bags that deserve to die?"

Filled with anger, confusion, and pain, she sat on the floor and took out her notebook and pen. She began writing out a list, which she entitled "Everyone I would rather have died instead of my grandmother."

Raphael observed from Maria's closet. He did not make it a habit, but having spent so much time down on Earth, he had caught a few movies in his time. One of his favorites was the *Star Wars* Saga. In fact, he once engaged in a heated discussion with one of his guardian angel friends—Morris—over which were the best of the *Stars Wars* movies: the new Trilogy or the Originals.

"Good story line and character development beats overblown special effects every time." Raphael insisted.

Morris did not agree.

As Raphael reflected on the *Star Wars* Saga, he wanted to yell out to Maria, "Don't do it! Don't go to the dark side!"

As he watched Maria crying in anger he thought, *Maybe it will be best if I just give Maria the letter from her grandmother. I don't know that my cheesy Star Wars musings would help her out right now.*

Maria put down her notebook with her "I would rather" Death List. She lay down on the floor of her bedroom and drifted off into an erratic dream state.

"Now's my chance," Raphael whispered.

He delivered the letter then took up temporary residence back in Maria's closet while he waited for her to awake. He did not have to wait long. Maria abruptly awoke seemingly from a bad dream. She wiped the drool gathered on her cheek. As she did, she noticed an envelope that had apparently slipped out of her notebook.

"What's this?" she questioned as she ripped right into the envelope.

She frantically pulled out the letter and began to read. Her body slowly slipped back to the floor as she continued reading in utter amazement. As she read, she could hear her grandma's voice uttering every word in her strong southern accent.

Dear Maria,

Well isn't this something? Your ol' grandma gets a chance to speak her mind one more time! I don't how this is happening, but I believe I know why. I have been told I can only leave my thoughts with one person, of whom I am also told that person will be the only one who can see my words in this letter. You know me...I asked all kinds of questions and this good ol' boy that helped me said that if anyone else looks at it, all they will see is an empty page. Don't know how that works, but I believed him. So, why don't you just keep this to yourself. Don't want anyone thinking you're crazy or something.

Alrighty then, let's get down to business. First off, I know you're sad and probably a little angry, but know this...I went with no pain or sorrow. Just died of old age! So while you may miss me, remember that I lived a full life and was ready to go.

Next thing, you know your Gram has plenty of opinions and I'm not afraid to share 'em and there are a lot of people I'd love to say a few things to, but I chose to leave my last words with you...my Maria. So listen up to what your ol' Grammy has to tell you.

Maria, there are people in this world who bring a black cloud with them everywhere they go. They literally darken a room with their presence...don't be that person. I love your mother, she's my daughter, but she has never learned how to let go, how to forgive, how to just accept people, love 'em and move on even when you don't agree with 'em or they've hurt you real bad.

Loving people can be a lot of work, but so is being bitter. The biggest difference between the two is not how that affects others, but how it affects you! Loving people opens up your heart for God's love to flow through you; bitterness just stops you up. Life is too short for holding stuff against folks. What a waste of time! We all have twenty-four hours to live each day, and they can never be gotten back. When they're gone, they're gone. But the thing is that those twenty-four hours turn into days, then them days turns into weeks, and them weeks become months then years and then...they become a lifetime.

Once you get in the habit of living a certain way, it's real hard to change that, but it can be done. If you find yourself being angry all the time, try being happy for awhile and see how that fits you. If you do it for a few hours...well...you keep it up and before you know it, you've lived an entire lifetime being joyful and bringing that happiness into the lives of others.

On the other hand, you get in the habit of always being grumpy and critical of everyone and always mad about something...well, before you know it you've lived a whole life as a grumpy ol' critic that no one wants to be around. Believe, me...I know! You see when I was about your age—maybe a lil' bit older—I lost my daddy; he would have been your great granddad. He was a great man. Always positive and optimistic, believing that things would always get better—even during really bad times.

Back when I was a kid, we didn't have a lot. We was poor...I mean really poor! Sometimes we wouldn't have a whole lot to eat and I would hear Momma crying in the kitchen, worried about what she was going to feed us kids. Then Daddy would go in there and start rummaging through the empty cabinets and he'd find a 'tater or two and maybe some beans. And then he would start hugging Momma and dancing around talking about the gourmet feast we were going to dine on that night. He would shoo Momma out of the kitchen and tell her to get the table ready for a special dining experience. Now, I don't know how he did it, but he would turn that bit a nothing into a wonderful stew or a casserole. He made sure Momma used the "nice" plates and silverware and he would light up some candles he had hidden away and we would all sit down to the "fancy" dinner Daddy had stirred up. He would always say grace before the meal, and I gotta be honest, not once did he sound ungrateful...not once. Daddy seemed to have a real good relationship with God. He talked to Him a lot. Maybe that's how Daddy was able to make those wonderful dinners...maybe he had some angelic help sent from above. Anyways, when my daddy died, I felt like I died. I got real angry: angry at people, angry at God, and angry at myself. For some reason I couldn't quit feeling guilty about my dad dying, I guess I felt like God was trying to punish me or something, so I was always trying to figure out what I'd done wrong.

I spent several years that way. I got real critical and didn't want anyone to get close to me. I held everything against everyone. If you crossed me once, well...you went on my list and I didn't want nothing to do with you ever again. I got real negative 'bout life and I became one of those people I told you not to become. Then one day, when I was about twenty-nine...something happened that changed my outlook forever.

Your grandpa and I had been married for about eight years and already had three kids, one of them being your mother. I really don't know what your grandpa saw in me that made him want to marry me. Looking back...I wouldn't have wanted to marry myself as miserable as I was! I guess I was pretty enough and your Grandpa liked the way I looked. Anyways, I had gotten up early on a beautiful spring morning in early June. It was a Saturday, so the kids were sleeping in...so was your Grandpa. I had gone outside to feed the chickens and gather up some eggs for breakfast. We had a nice little farm that helped provide us all that we needed to survive. We always had plenty to eat and we never went hungry. I went back inside and began to make breakfast. As I began to cook, I knew that I wouldn't need to go wake anyone up; the wonderful aroma would take care of that for me.

I cracked open an egg and then I heard little Emma crying. I just thought that everyone was beginning to stir. Then I heard her again, but her cry didn't seem to be coming from her room, it sounded like it was coming from outside. I stepped out on the front porch and now I could hear her screaming, but it seemed like her scream was moving away. "Oh no," I thought, "She's fallen in the creek!" I yelled for your grandpa and then began to run across our property down to the creek bank. I was thinking about how the creek is what sold us on the property. We loved taking the kids down to play in it, and I even washed the clothes in it sometimes. This was our first year there, and we had not realized how much the water rose when the spring rains came. I got down to the creek and screamed Emma's name. She was now quite a ways away. I could barely see her little head bobbing up and down in the water. The current was moving fast and I couldn't keep up with her.

I ran back to the house and your Grandpa Ed was already on the porch. I quickly screamed out what was happening, and he got the key to his old truck and began to drive off down the road. I wanted to go with him, but I knew I needed to stay back with the other kids. I was flooded with thoughts of how God was punishing me again, and my heart was filled with anger and I began to yell aloud toward the sky, "Why! You took my dad, and now You want my little girl to? What has she done to deserve this?" I yelled many things. In my mind, lil' Emma was already gone. I had no faith that she would be ok. Then, as the other kids ran out of the house asking what was going on, a strange thing happened.

Out of my mouth came these words, "Your dad went to get Emma. She fell in the creek, but God sent His angels to save her. She's gonna be just fine, and they'll be back here in just a bit. C'mon kids, let's go eat breakfast." As we went back into the house, I couldn't stop thinking about what I had just said. Where did those words come from? Then it hit me, those are the words my Daddy would have said. He would have declared a miracle in the midst of a possible tragedy. He would have brought a sense of peace and assurance where none existed. As I began to serve the other two kids their breakfast I realized something. After my daddy died, I had become so bitter and angry that I had left the best of who he was behind. I hadn't allowed my daddy to live on through me. Not only had his body been buried, but I had unintentionally buried the best of who he was. He would be heartbroken to know that I had become a bitter ol' cynic that made everyone miserable. That was not who he was and that is not who he raised me to be.

I made sure the kids were settled then went back outside and knelt down on the bottom porch stairs. I looked up to God and prayed a simple prayer. I tried to do it like I had seen my daddy do it so many times before. I don't remember exactly what I said, but essentially I told God I was sorry and that I would do anything if He would save my little Emma. My daddy had always taught me that if I made a vow to anyone, especially God, I had better keep it. With that in mind, I vowed to God that I was ready to change and ready to let go of years of bitterness and unforgiveness. I vowed that from that day forward, I was going to be a different person. I asked Him to heal my heart and help me to hold onto the memory of my father but let go of the pain, sorrow and anger. Then once again, I asked Him to please save my little Emma.

I'm not quite sure how long I was knelt down at the porch, but as soon as I began to get up, I heard the sound of Ed's truck pulling up the road. The other kids ran out of the house and we all ran toward the truck. My heart began to thump rapidly as a sense of panic surged through my body. I did not see Emma. Ed was alone in the truck.

"Oh no," I said, "She's gone…my little Emma is gone!"

I was breathless as I fell to the ground unable to even cry as my emotions now turned to shock. Then Ed put his hand on me and said, "Get up, honey! Emma's fine! She's just fine! Dr. Proctor has her and is driving her to the clinic to check her out. I just came back to get you and the kids. So come on!"

I leapt to my feet and threw my arms around him and kissed him right on his mouth! I know, Maria…not a nice thought for you, but we were younger and unwrinkled back then if that helps you out.

In those days, it was common for your kids to just ride in the back of the truck; so they jumped in and away we went. As we drove to the clinic, your Grandpa Ed told me how he had driven down to the Bridge at the end of Winkler's Pass. He got out and began to wait and see if Emma was still coming down the creek. Then he looked up at a tree and there was Emma hanging from a branch. Her little pants were hooked on the limb and she was crying as she dangled in the wind. Ed said that the branch was too far above the water for her to have just accidentally been hooked by it. He said someone must've bent the branch down and caught her on it, but no one was around when he arrived.

"Must've been some kind of miracle," he said.

"Must have been!" I said with a smile as tears of joy poured down my face.

Emma was just fine. Not one scratch on her. Maria, I'm sure you are wondering why you never heard this story and who Emma was, because none of your aunts have that name. Well, the reasons why are just plain stupid. To start with, none of your aunts were named Emma...your mother was. Her full name was Emma Louise, but by the time you were born, she had come to be known as just Louise. She hated the name Emma, so we just stopped using it. Then your mother actually had her name officially changed. Who ever heard of such a thing? As far as the story, we stopped telling it because of your mother also. Somehow she didn't see it as a miracle story. She just thought it was embarrassing. So, by the time you were born, we had stopped telling it. I don't know why we let your momma control us so much. For some reason, she is the only one who was ever able to shut me up! It's a shame too, 'cause it's a good story! It truly was a miracle and a good thing she made it or you wouldn't even be alive.

I have wondered many times why my Daddy died and Emma was saved. I have no answer. But I do know this; that day I vowed to change with God's help, and well...I changed with God's help.

Maria, my life has been full of wonder and great blessing. I have had the privilege of living through so many events that you now know as history—that is if you paid attention in school! I was alive to hear the infamous "I have a Dream" speech by Martin Luther King in 1967. I witnessed Neil Armstrong and Buzz Aldrin be the first men on the moon. As a little girl, I lived through World War II and then was alive to witness the Berlin wall fall in 1989. I mention these few historic events to emphasize to you that the life you live today will be the history of tomorrow.

I want you to know, Maria, my fondest historical memories are not known by most people, but they have always been treasured in my heart. Many of these memories include days and moments like September 17, 1990, at 3:31 a.m.—the day and moment you were born. From the moment you came to be, my life changed. I love all of my grandchildren, so please don't tell the others...but you were always my favorite! I can still remember your cry; it was as unique as your personality. I can remember every nurse wanting to sneak in to see and hold you. And that never changed! You always lit up a room with your presence, and oh...that smile! Could there be a more beautiful display of joy in all the world? Though I must say that I saw that smile less and less over the last few years and I know my leaving isn't going to help.

Maria, please listen to your grandmother right now. You are a wonderfully unique person that has the ability to affect everyone around you with your contagious joy, love, and spontaneity.

Don't let my passing make you a bitter, mean woman like what happened to me when my daddy passed on. Live life full of expectancy, and when disappointment comes embrace it as part of the journey and let it make you stronger, more compassionate, more kind and understanding. Don't let troubles and difficulties make you hard-hearted, untrusting, judgmental and critical...that's no way to live! You only have so much time upon the earth, make your minutes count. Live life in the moment not in the regrets of yesterday or the worries for tomorrow.

I leave knowing that I ran my race well. I ran hard. I loved with all of my heart, I gave fully of myself and my greatest desire is for those I leave behind to do the same. I love you, my Maria. Now you let God heal your heart like your grandma did and you get out there and be that girl that lights up the room and brings joy to everyone you meet. That's who you are and who you were made to be, don't let anyone, even me, change that. I'll be praying for you!

Love,

Grandma Francis

CHAPTER 9

Richard attempted to regain control of the car, but it was too late. He spun across the median in the road and hit the guardrail. The rail collapsed under the impact as Richard and his rusted out 92 Ford Tempo flew over the cliff. Richard knew he was going to die; however, he was too inebriated to care. The car flipped over several trees and came to rest on a large serrated rock. The impact caused the gas tank to rupture. Moments later Richard and his Ford Tempo erupted in flames. No one heard his screams. No one saw him die.

"But if I'm dead, then why is someone reaching their hand in to help me?" Richard said aloud.

"Come on," Raphael declared. "You've got some unfinished business."

"Then, I'm not dead?"

"Oh, you're dead! But there's someone who needs to live, and you're going to help!"

Raphael was surprised at his own tone and directness. His usual compassionate self that tried to bring understanding was absent.

Even an angel has his limits, he thought to himself. *I am not here by choice. I am here because the Commander ordered it and because Richard is being given a chance.*

The chance Richard was being given was not one for his own redemption; it was too late for that. This chance had everything to do with someone else.

Raphael explained the opportunity to Richard. He did not mince words or even pretend Richard had a choice. He was not giving him a choice.

Speak your last words and make them good...or else! Raphael thought.

He knew he did not have the authority for an "or else," but he sure wished he did. Richard was surprisingly cooperative. It is amazing how sobering death can be.

His mother was crying. The phone was ringing. Someone was knocking at the door. His dog was barking, and some neighbor woman he did not know was giving him a hug. In the midst of all the commotion, Justin felt numb and emotionless.

"A drunk driver had an accident and his dad is dead." That is what he continued to hear his mother say. Between answering the door and talking on the phone, his mother kept telling him she was sorry.

I'm not sorry, Justin thought. *A drunk is dead. So what if he was my dad. Who cares? Why is my mom crying? She doesn't care. Why is she acting like she cares? Nobody cares! A drunk driver killed my dad? Why is she telling people that? My dad was the drunk driver and he killed himself. Serves him right. He's better off dead. We are all better off!*

Aunt Norma interrupted his thoughts as she embraced him with a hug and another "I'm so sorry!"

Justin let go of Aunt Norma as his mind swept him back into his private thoughts. *Why is everyone acting as if they are sorry? Don't they know what happened in this house just two days ago? Don't they know the torment that happened behind these walls?*

His mom knew.

Why does she act like she loved him? All they did was fight and two nights ago, my 'wonderful' father had a knife at my mom's throat. And then, when it was over, she made excuses for him like she always did.

Drunken arguments were normal in Justin's house. What bothered him though was no one did anything about it.

His mom would tell him, "Honey, it's not your father, it's the alcohol. You just need to be patient with him, he will change; you just have to give him time."

Justin waited fourteen years. Nothing changed.

While everyone gathered in the front of the house, Raphael snuck into Justin's room through an open window. He laid the letter on his pillow and turned to leave.

I hope this helps, Raphael thought.

This had been a difficult assignment for Raphael. He knew what took place in this house. He knew the torment that had gone on.

He also knew the last words Richard said to his son: "Boy... you're gonna be just like me! That's right...pay attention to your ol' dad, 'cause you're gonna be just like him! Here, take a drink. Get used to the taste because this here bottle is the best this world has to offer. This bottle will be your best friend. In time, it will be your only friend."

Justin did take a drink. What Richard did not know was that it was not Justin's first; that came two years before. Justin had already started down his father's dark path.

Raphael tried not to think about it.

Why can't I just do my job? Why am I getting so emotionally involved?

A hundred different thoughts swirled through his mind.

Why couldn't Richard get some help? Why don't parents realize how much their bad decisions affect their kids? Why does the Commander love them so much? Don't they realize that one day their lives will end? They sure don't live like they care. Why don't they realize how much the Commander loves them? It sure would make them live different if they really knew Him!

He paused for a moment as he saw Justin coming down the hall.

Raphael looked up as he whispered, "Commander, I know angels are not supposed to pray—that is a gift You have given to Your human creation—but, if I could just this once... Please let Justin be all right. Please let him find You! Please Commander, please."

Justin entered his room with that strange feeling he was not alone. He was not. Raphael just had to stick around. Justin threw himself down on his bed. He was not crying. He was not smiling. He was not...

"Hey, what is this?"

Justin picked up the envelope. A puzzled look plundered his face. The envelope fell to the floor as Justin began to read.

Well Justin…

I am dead. I wouldn't blame you if you were happy. I never was much of a dad, was I? It seemed like at one time I could've been. Unfortunately, at some point I picked up "the bottle" and never put it down again. Ended up killing me. Thank God no one else was hurt. Strange for you to hear me say "God"? Well, I do believe in Him—especially now—just never got around to knowing Him. But I think He must know you! Why else would I be given this chance to speak to you one more time? Apparently, this is important; at least this guy that I think works for God sure thinks so.

I've never done anything important, so this will be a first. I haven't been given a lot of time to think about what I want to say so I hope I get it right. I realize that nothing I say is going to help me now…too late. This is all for you. I don't know how to fix what I've done to you. I realize that I may have already killed you on the inside; for this, I am sorry.

I know it's been hard being a kid with a dad like me. You know, I wasn't always like this; I was a kid once! Hard to believe, right? I can remember my dad, your grandpa. He was always traveling…trying to sell something. I was never quite sure what it was that he sold; I just know that he was gone a lot. But I remember a time he was there. It was my eleventh birthday. I was looking forward to that day for months. My mom, your grandma, was planning a big party for me. She invited all the neighborhood kids and all the kids from my class. I was so excited. But I was most excited about my dad being there. He was coming home from a sales trip and had promised to bring me a great present. I could not wait.

Well the day came and the house was filled. My mom had really outdone herself. There was cake and games, and everyone seemed to be having a great time. I couldn't believe it. I wasn't a very popular kid so this was my big chance. Kids were actually being nice to me and saying, "Cool party, Rich!" I was smiling. I was having fun. My life was good. To make it even better, Mom told me that my dad had called and said he was going to be home in about ten minutes. He was in town and had just stopped to fuel up the car.

My mom got the cake ready and was waiting to light the candles when my dad came through the door. He had a big package. It was all wrapped up in red and white striped paper with a bow tied to the top. Looked like a toy store clerk had helped Dad out. I didn't care. I just couldn't wait to see what was inside! It was too small to be a bike, but too big to be a baseball bat and glove. I was sure it had to be the coolest gift ever. All of the kids gathered around the table, as I got ready to blow out my candles. Everyone was talking about the "big gift" my dad had brought. I felt like a celebrity.

We ate the cake and ice cream, and then my mom announced it was time to open presents. I said I wanted to save dad's present for last. I ripped through gift after gift. A frisbee. A yo-yo. A basketball. Wonderful gift after wonderful gift. But I was sure, none could compare to Dad's big gift.

My dad hadn't always been there for me, but now...as I turned eleven he was helping me become a man. He brought the gift that had everyone talking. I thought it might be a BB gun! In that moment, I was the coolest kid on the block. I didn't want the moment to ever end. I wanted to stop time and just live with all of those kids and my family looking at me and the big gift and thinking how cool I was, how fortunate I was, how wonderful my life was, how cool my dad was.

I was the king...then I opened the box.

I took my time taking off the wrapping paper and removing the bow. I opened up the cardboard top with expectant care. I reached inside. Embarrassment filled my face. I could not believe what I was looking at.

"Go ahead, Richie, show everyone what you got!" my mom said.

All I could think was, "Did she know what was inside... was she in on the biggest humiliation of my young life? And if so...I hated her as much or more than I hated my dad in that moment." I would never live this down.

Everyone kept yelling for me to show them the "present." I don't know how long I waited before the big "reveal." All I know is I wanted to disappear and pretend this moment never happened.

My mom grew impatient and pushed past me with a look of disgust. She reached into the box and pulled out the gift with great enthusiasm. Everyone else tried to hold back the laughter for all of three or four seconds. But laughter was the correct response. And laugh they did; for the rest of my school years. Boy can kids be cruel.

After that day, I had a new and permanent nickname, "Teddy." My Dad had given me the biggest Teddy bear I had ever seen. It was brown with pink trim, pink bow, and pink booties. He said he won the bear in a sales contest. He told my mom, "I thought it would be the perfect gift and it didn't cost me any money."It was the perfect gift... for a little girl! But I was an eleven-year-old boy who desperately wanted to be a man, who wanted to be accepted and liked. I was a boy who longed for my dad to lead me into manhood. Instead...my dad crushed me.

I never quite recovered from that moment. That stupid bear represented something. It represented the first time my private hell became public. My dad was not cool like he appeared to be for all of about forty-five minutes that day. My dad was not nice, as he wanted everyone to think. My dad was an angry, cruel drunk who abused his wife and kids. He wanted to embarrass me on my birthday.

Until that day, I had always been able to keep private life and public life separate. After that, it just didn't seem to matter. The truth is, everyone in life faces some kind of pain or disappointment, my problem was I never dealt with it. Instead, I let it build up until my life was filled with nothing but pain and darkness. I didn't know how to get out.

Eventually, I just wanted to ease the pain. So, when I was sixteen years old, I turned to alcohol. This was shortly after my mom and dad divorced. Your grandpa was cheating on your grandma—not hard to believe as often as he was away. It was funny, your grandma put up with the anger, and verbal and physical abuse, but she would not put up with your grandpa cheating.

After that, my mom tried her best to carry on, but she didn't know how to deal with disappointment or pain either. I am not making excuses, but I never had good role models in my life. I did have some that tried—coaches, counselors, even the local pastor—but I always pushed them away. That's the thing about being in pain on the inside. You can grow accustomed to it and when someone tries to help you, you reject them because you do not want to let go of the pain. Somehow, it becomes part of your identity. You don't know who you'd be if you weren't hurt, cynical and disappointed. Once it becomes part of who you are, you make choices that deaden the pain but never deal with the issues. What you don't realize is how much your choices begin to ruin the lives of others.

I was always so consumed with my own personal pain that I was blind to the pain I was constantly inflicting on other people. I see things so clearly now that I am dead, and it's too late.

Justin, I need to say something that you need to hear. My life, as much as it was a life, is over; but yours is not!

I know I hurt you and brought a lot of pain into your life. For that, I am sorry.

I am sorry for all of the names I called you. I am sorry for all of the times I told you, you would never amount to anything. I am sorry for telling you that you were a waste of space. I am sorry for telling you that you were an accident that I never wanted. I am sorry for spitting on you.

I am sorry for hitting you in the face. For hitting you with a bat. For throwing beer bottles at you. For locking you in the closet. Justin...I am sorry you had to watch as I beat your mother. I am sorry the only time I spent with you I was drunk.

Justin, I can never remove the hurt and pain that I poured out upon you. I can't even ask you to forgive me, I don't deserve it. If you do forgive me, don't do it for me—it's too late—do it for yourself. Do it to let me go and move on.

Well, I'm about done but I need you to hear these last words...for they are the last words I will ever say...to anyone.

Justin, you did not deserve any of this.

You did not deserve my verbal abuse. You did not deserve the physical abuse. There is nothing wrong with you. You are a wonderful kid who had a terrible dad. I never dealt with my pain. Instead, I tried to drown it in alcohol. When that didn't work, I took it out on you and your mother.

Justin, your life doesn't have to be like mine. Everyone has pain; everyone experiences disappointment. But you don't have to let it destroy you. You can choose to listen to people who really want to help you...like your mom. I always mocked her for wanting to go to church and called you a "sissy" when you went. Justin, I was wrong. Listen to your mom; she knows what she is talking about. Listen to the people who want to help you. Know that what I did was wrong and is not the way people are supposed to treat one another.

I made my choices and now...it is too late. My life is over. Yours is just beginning. Do whatever you have to do to be healed of the pain.

Justin, I did what I said I would never do...I became just like my dad...a mean, angry drunk. Please...I am begging you...do not be like me.

I hope to never see you again, because where I think I'm going is no place for you.

Sincerely,

Your dad

Justin sat on his bed stunned. A strange silence infected the room. It was as if someone hit the mute button and all of the noise in the house disappeared. He heard nothing but his own heartbeat. Then...it started. He could not remember the last time this had happened. Justin cried.

As the tears flowed, Justin closed his eyes and did something else he had not done for a long time. He prayed: one simple prayer.

"Help me...God if You are out there...if You are real...help me...please."

As the tears continued, an aroma of peace filled the room. Raphael smiled. He knew this presence. *The Commander is here.*

Years of confusion, guilt, and shame poured out with every tear. With one honest prayer the healing process had begun.

Raphael brushed by Justin unseen. He closed his eyes and said, "Thank You, Commander! Thank You!"

Raphael observed many times how difficult it was for humans to overcome abuse. He thought about the difficult journey Justin faced. However, Justin's heart had been touched. The Commander was already at work. This was His specialty: taking what others had broken and making it whole again.

He really is the only one that can heal their broken hearts, Raphael thought. *I sure wish more people would let the Commander heal their brokenness.*

As he began his assent to his next assignment, he could not help but speak aloud, "Commander, You are amazing!"

CHAPTER 10

John was grateful for the tinted windows as the limousine rolled into the cemetery. Even his enormous wire-rimmed sunglasses could not hide his lack of emotion. He was truly devoid of all feelings. This place did that to him; it was all so déjà vu. He had been here four times in recent years: once for each of his siblings and once for each of his parents. To say he had known tragedy would have been an understatement.

As he vacantly stared out at the endless rows of headstones, memories began to replay in his head. He remembered the day his father died—heart attack. He could vividly recall his father slumped over in the backyard with the lawn mower still running. They had a big yard and his dad never wanted to purchase a riding mower. He insisted on using the push mower.

"Good exercise," he used to say.

Nobody heard him cry for help that day. Dad had disabled the automatic shut off because he did not like restarting the mower every time he needed to move something. Because of this, John and his mother never thought anything of the lawn mower continuing to run for almost an hour before it ran out of gas.

"I should have been mowing that day," John brooded.

For someone who was only twenty-nine years old, John had many regrets. He regretted not being at the lake the day his sister drowned. He regretted not being in the car the day his mother crashed. He especially regretted not being with his older brother the day he died. A police officer who was pursuing a criminal on the run mistakenly shot him down.

His brother came into the family through adoption; however, John had never known a day without him. Julio had joined their family before John was born.

John's parents were benevolent people who would assist anyone. Julio became an orphan after his mother abandoned him at three years old. John's mom, Anita, worked with Julio's mother at a homeless shelter. One day, Julio's mom just disappeared. Anita offered to take care of Julio until his mom returned; she never returned. Of course, John never knew these details until he was in his teens.

His grandfather—John Levitz Senior—told him many things. His grandfather was not one to keep secrets. Other than his father, there was no other man on the planet that John loved more. John was proud to carry the same name as his grandfather and his father. He was John Levitz the III. Everybody called him JB though; short for John Bryan.

JB could not remember who asked him to speak at his grandfather's funeral. He did say yes though and he did his best. Honoring his grandfather was effortless; he was an easy man to honor. However, doing it without breaking down, that was difficult. He made it about five minutes in and then was unable to finish. One of his grandfather's oldest living friends—George—came up and gave him a reassuring hug. He then took the microphone and finished the service. JB was grateful.

Now he just had to get out of the limo and make it through the short graveside committal. He would not break down and cry. He was emotionally numb. As the limo pulled up to the gravesite, JB put on his shades, took a deep breath, and stepped out into the crowd. As he walked toward the casket he lifted up a silent prayer, *Lord, give me the strength to do this one more time.*

Raphael observed from a distance as one after another, people left the gravesite. Most approached JB before leaving and offered a hug or a word of encouragement. JB politely received whatever they offered and thanked everyone for coming.

Soon, JB was alone. No one left but him and the limo driver. He started to leave but decided to visit his parents' graves instead. They were only a few rows over. The limo driver looked at his watch as he gave JB a nod and a wave indicating to take all the time he needed.

The driver smirked as he mused aloud, "Take your time, sir; take your time. I'm getting paid by the hour."

JB stopped in front of the graves of his mother and father. It was raining and he did not have an umbrella. However, he did not seem to care that he was getting drenched from head to toe. He stood motionless for almost an hour. Raphael moved closer as he became concerned with JB's unnervingly inert condition.

Raphael was not ready for what happened next.

JB went from being totally still to erupting like a dormant volcano that suddenly woke up. He violently began to run around kicking and hitting the head stones of his parents and siblings, as well as anything else that happened to be nearby. Trees, flowers in vases, other headstones, and even squirrels were not safe.

"Why! Why! Why!" he screamed. With every "why" JB annunciated his frustration by kicking a headstone or throwing some flowers.

After ten minutes, his pent-up emotions shifted from this physical display into a verbal tirade, which seemed directed toward God.

"WHY! Why did You let this happen? Well, You got my whole family now, so You might as well come get me. Here I am, go ahead and let the lightning fall! I'm no good down here anymore. I don't even want to be here. I want to be with my family! You've got everyone with You that I love, so c'mon, come and get me!"

JB discovered he did have more tears as he continued, "What have I done to deserve this? Why my whole family? Why! Tell me why? If You can't answer me then please just strike me down... please...I'm begging You, take me now!"

JB fell to his knees, and his head collapsed into the mud. His tears flowed out mixing with the rain. He slapped at the water multiple times while cries of anguish continued to spill out.

He then looked up while expelling one wordless cry, "AAWWWWW!"

He staggered to his feet. With his entire body shaking, he continued to stumble around uncontrollably. He looked up at the sky and screamed, "Well, if You're not going to do it, then I'll just do it for You!"

JB revealed the pistol he had been hiding in his interior suit-jacket pocket.

He waved it up in the air, "You had no problem killing the rest of my family, but I'll tell You what...I'll take care of this one for You!"

He lifted the gun to his head and put his finger on the trigger.

Raphael quickly moved closer as he dismissed every protocol ever given to him.

"Where's that driver?" he said.

The driver had fallen asleep about thirty minutes earlier and missed JB's entire breakdown.

"I know I am not supposed to get involved, but how can I stand by and watch this?" Raphael fretted.

Without further thought of personal consequence, he soared out and over JB's head. JB was shaking as his finger stroked the trigger. Raphael zoomed up and positioned himself directly above JB.

JB lifted his head and looked directly into the falling rain. He let out one more scream as he pushed the gun hard against his right temple, closed his eyes, and pulled the trigger. Raphael rocketed down and knocked the gun out of JB's hand at the very same moment. The bullet zoomed upward towards grey skies as the gun fell into a puddle of mud.

Raphael did not realize that the traumatic events had caused him to no longer be invisible. He landed a few feet in front of JB. Their eyes met and JB again stood motionless; his mouth and body seemingly frozen in time.

"Where did you come from?" JB asked.

Raphael looked down at himself realizing he was completely visible, "Look, JB…"

"Who are you and how do you know my name?" JB asked.

Raphael was in shock at his own behavior. *I need to say something, but what am I going to say? I need to say as little as possible,* he thought.

"Listen… I cannot answer all of your questions. In fact, I should not even be talking to you and you should not even be seeing me. I just need to give you something and then I am going to disappear."

"Wait a second. You still haven't told me who you are and… give me what? What do you mean disappear?"

Raphael could not remember ever being this nervous. *I am going to be in so much trouble!* he thought to himself.

"Here, just take this." Raphael pulled an envelope from behind his back and handed it to JB. "I am sorry, I have to go."

"But, who are you?"

JB looked down at the envelope and saw his name, his complete name: John Bryan Levitz the III.

"Who is this from? Why are you giving this to me? Hey, wait! Don't go!"

When JB looked down again, Raphael disappeared. As he sped away from the cemetery, he noticed that his appointment notebook was flashing. Not only was it flashing, it was flashing RED. He opened the notebook and saw a new appointment highlighted. It said he had a meeting with Michael the head warrior angel.

"A meeting with an archangel?" Raphael almost fell out of the sky. *This can't be good.*

Down below, JB ducked under a tree to get out of the rain. He ran his hands along every side of the envelope as he surveyed the landscape around him. He wondered about what just happened and where the mysterious stranger went. His biggest question was, what was in the envelope and who was it from.

He pulled out his pocketknife and cut open the side of the envelope, as his grandfather had taught him to do years ago. He removed the letter and almost lost his breath.

"Grandpa? This is from you? But how?"

JB looked around one more time. The mysterious stranger was gone. He leaned against the tree and began to read.

JB,

There are no words to express how sad I am that you are left alone again. Believe me; I would rather be there with you right now. I know that you have seen more than your fair share of death and hardship, but you must remember that you still have the gift of life and that is a gift you should cherish.

I want you to know that I am moving on from this life with very few regrets. My life has been full and meaningful. The good

Lord above blessed me with a wonderful wife and kids. He allowed me to see and experience great changes in our world and even to survive some unbelievable disasters.

My only regret was that I outlived your beautiful grandmother and your mom and dad. However, after your mom and dad passed on, I recieved an incredible gift in the midst of terrible darkness and pain. I got you. Now I know that you came to live with me so that I could finish raising you, but you will never know how much you gave back to me. You gave this old man a renewed sense of purpose in his old age.

Yeah son, you were definitely a gift of God to me. What I want you to understand now is that the good Lord above is not finished with you yet. You still got some living to do! Now I know you may be mad at Him and you may be asking why all of this has happened. I don't blame you, you're only human. I sure have a lot of questions myself; and now I wish I could answer yours, but I can't. But I do know for sure that God loves you. I really think He tries to let us know how much He loves us every day. He just generally does it subtly: a sunrise, a fresh breath of air, an unexpected smile. JB, don't let the hardships of life rob you of the actual gift of life. Remember, we'd never know what good was, if we hadn't seen bad. I mean, think about it, light is meaningless if there ain't no darkness for it to shine into.

JB, I know you miss me, but I don't want you to grieve for me. Instead, I want you to honor me. Honor me by going out and living! Honor me by pursuing your dreams. Honor me by overcoming the hardships you have faced with a new sense of purpose. Honor me by being a man of integrity and character in a world that has lost its ability to define these traits, much less live them. Honor me by giving other people hope in the midst of their darkness. Honor me by being who God made you to be and making no apology for it. Honor me, your mom and dad, and your brother and sister, by living a life worthy of our deaths. You have been kept alive for a reason. Make your life count enough for us all.

I was given this last chance to speak to you and I want to make it count. So I have made you a list. Now I know I am famous for my lists and you're probably laughing right now just thinking about it. Well, if you're laughing then good. I want you to laugh when you think about me. You've had enough of grieving, so go ahead and laugh your head off! Please, I insist!

Now back to what I was talking about, the list. This list is some random thoughts, some wisdom, or lessons (or whatever you want to call them) that I wanted to leave with you. It is my way of reminding you of everything I attempted to instill in you. In addition, it is my attempt at living on through you. I've done my part on this journey, son, now it's your turn. Take the baton from me and all of the family and finish the race. Make us proud and remember that we will be watching!

I hope to be seeing the good Lord soon and I am going to ask Him to keep an extra good eye on you for me and continue to help you on your way.

Enjoy the List,

Grandpa John

Grandpa's List:

No matter how dark it gets, look up and keep on staring; sooner or later light will appear.

Seek to be content. For the content man is free to pursue his dreams for the right reasons; while the discontent man will always be driven by selfishness, greed, and fear.

Do not live for your epitaph, live for your legacy. Your epitaph shows up when you are dead; your legacy starts today.

The difference between a good hunting dog and a bad hunting dog is his sense of smell. (When you are facing a situation in life and something don't "smell" right, just remember you come from a long line of good "hunting dogs.")

If you continually live without forgiving others, you will never genuinely live.

Seek to see the potential in people more than you see their faults.

Remember that you will always stand out if you will simply do this: be kind!

The future belongs to those who are willing to risk their tomorrows today.

When you embrace your destination, you find peace in your journey even when the next step is not clear.

Always remember, failure is a teacher, mediocrity is a prison.

Having character will cost you, but compromise will destroy you.

Putting forth maximum effort for the best possible temporary existence we can create does not change the fact it is still temporary. Live for what is eternal, live for what matters.

Live life in the moment, because in a moment, life will be gone.

Success is not about what you accumulate. Success is about how you live.

Love that lasts is more about sacrifice than about a feeling.

**JB, this list is not finished yet, so why don't you go ahead and finish it for me. Thanks!*

CHAPTER 11

The Meeting

Appointment: Meet with Michael the Archangel @ 2:15 p.m. Eastern Earth Time.

Location: You will be contacted.

Raphael stared at his notebook as he waited for Michael to arrive. He had received word of the meeting place a few hours prior. He now sat on a rock in the middle of a clearing in the upper tundra of northern Canada. There were no human inhabitants for miles. It was 2:05 p.m. Eastern Earth Time. Michael, known for his punctuality, would be here at any moment. Raphael figured that was why the Commander always gave him or Gabriel the important jobs. That fact made Raphael even more nervous.

Raphael began to replay the entire JB incident. His thoughts were stacking up like unused clutter in a meticulously well kept home:

Why did I do it? I have never really gotten involved. I mean, I have had a few minor slip-ups, but nothing major. I cannot believe this, one incident in three earth years and the Commander sends Michael to deal with me. I guess I should have just allowed JB to take his own life, but how could I? Is that really what the Commander wanted? Maybe now they will find someone more qualified for this and I can be reassigned! Though I must admit, I have kind of grown to like this job. I have seen some people do and say some incredible things. However, I do not think they truly understand their true capacity to love. It seems to be one of those characteristics the Commander gave them that they struggle to unleash. Maybe it is because that kind of deep love is only revealed when they get to know the Commander. Not very many ever take the time to do that. Many want to know about Him, and a few strive to be experts concerning Him, but few really know Him.

"Greetings, Raphael."

Startled, Raphael slipped off the rock. He embarrassingly jumped up, spun around in midair, and landed directly in front of Michael. As he came to attention and saluted, he could not help but note one additional archangel advantage: total stealth mode.

"Sir, it is an honor...it is a pleasure to...well a...nice to meet with you...sir."

Raphael had rehearsed this moment repeatedly and already it was not going the way he planned. He was nervous; when he was nervous, his mouth did not always cooperate.

Michael stared down at Raphael. His lack of response instilled an unnerving quiet. Raphael knew to look everyone he communicated with in the eye. It was a sign of confidence. The Commander hated arrogance but desired for all of His angels to operate with what He called "humble confidence." Right now, Raphael was having no problem with the humble part; however, in the presence of the mighty archangel Michael, any confidence he possessed vanished like socks in a dryer. He stood staring at anything but Michael.

He wondered why Michael was not talking. Seconds felt like hours.

Without warning or introduction, Michael spoke. "Raphael, I am not here to discuss anything."

"You're not?"

Raphael was not certain if he had thought the question or spoke it aloud. Apparently, it did not matter; Michael continued.

"The Commander does not send me to discuss issues, he sends me to deliver messages or... win battles."

Raphael was fine with this not being a discussion. He had nothing to say. He could take a one-sided conversation. However, he did hope Michael was there to deliver a message, because he did not want to be on the other end of a rumble with an archangel.

"On the record..." Michael said.

On the record? Raphael thought that was a bizarre way to start a message from the Commander.

Michael continued, "On the record, the Commander wants you to never do anything like that again. Other angels are already talking and it just does not look good if an angel—with what some consider a 'questionable' assignment—goes rogue and starts disobeying orders and taking matters into his own hands. That kind of thing can lead down the wrong path; I believe you know to what I'm referring."

Raphael nodded.

"You need to realize that even though your assignment is 'classified,' you are being watched. You may not believe this but there are others who are jealous of what you are doing."

Jealous? Raphael could not believe that any angel would be jealous of him. He wrestled with his assignment on a daily basis: since before his training, he harbored aspirations of working with one of the archangels in what he considered a "real job." He often thought of how incredible it would be to work with Michael and experience being on the front lines; or to soar with the archangel Gabriel as one of the messenger angels.

Raphael attempted to keep his eyes open and appear confident as he awaited the continuation of Michael's message from the Commander. Then, Michael's entire demeanor changed as he moved closer and knelt down in front of Raphael. He was now looking at Raphael eye to eye. This was quite a feat considering Michael was almost three times taller.

"Raphael, there is another part to the Commander's message, but...this is off the record, and this stays just between me, you, and the Commander."

Off the record? Raphael found it amusing that the Commander would say anything "off the record."

"Off the record, the Commander is extremely proud of you." Michael smiled a general's smile—stoic yet genuine and warm.

Raphael was speechless and tried not to embarrass himself by falling over again.

Michael continued, "The Commander knew what was in you and knew what you would do in that situation. It was His purpose for you to be there. Your action was not an accident. He has great plans for JB. The Commander is going to take everything JB has been through and use it to touch and change many lives. It is amazing to watch Him work. Even after all of these years in His service, I am still speechless at times."

Raphael wanted to pinch himself to see if he was dreaming. Michael the archangel was sharing his private thoughts about the Commander, with him. Raphael continued to stare in shocked disbelief.

Michael stepped down and gave Raphael a firm handshake, "I'll tell you what, Raphee, if the Commander didn't already have you tied up in this assignment that 'doesn't exist,' I would put in a request to have you on my squad. I could sure use more like you!"

Raphael, beaming, finally spoke with humble confidence, "Sir, thank you and please let the Commander know that I am, well…just tell Him thank you for me."

"I'll do that, but maybe you can just tell Him yourself. If you check your notebook there, I believe you will see that you have an appointment with the Commander next Tuesday at three. I believe He wants to talk to you about the success of your assignment and about the possibility of taking on an intern."

Again, Raphael was speechless. Even so, inside he was mulling over the word 'intern.'

"For now, Raph, let's just put this whole incident behind us, and for the sake of the other angels, pretend it never happened." Michael winked. "You keep up the good work!"

With that, Michael effortlessly soared upward, disappearing into the clouds.

Raphael could not stop smiling. He had been dreading this meeting, and just like that, it was over. For the first time since he had received this special assignment, Raphael genuinely appreciated his purpose.

CHAPTER 12

Conner Mason stepped out into the cold mid-winter air. A stifling chill traversed up his spine. A combination of thermal underwear, purple running suit, green sweat pants, and an old faded sweatshirt proclaimed his pursuit of warmth over style. A torn, knitted, grey hat and mismatched gloves completed his chaotic ensemble. A vision of fashion he was not; but he was warm and endeavoring to remain dedicated to his newest resolution. Conner made a vow to run two to three miles four days a week. So far, he had been faithful. Four months had gone by and he was still at it. Even his wife, Amber, was impressed with his commitment. She was not only impressed but she was also thrilled that he had lost twenty-five pounds. Conner was not obese, but he could definitely afford to lose a little weight. He had become very concerned with his health after numerous visits to the doctor revealed high cholesterol and the symptoms of clogged arteries. Conner was only forty-six.

Amber smiled and waved as Conner began his morning run. The Mason family resided on the outskirts of a small town in Western Colorado. While the town was in the valley, their home was up in the base of the Rocky Mountain range. Their property was exquisite: hidden away amongst an extraordinary display of evergreens and pine trees. A blanket of snow completed the picturesque scene. The closest home to them was almost a mile away.

Conner and Amber were high-school sweethearts. They followed each other to college and married during their junior year. Conner studied marketing and Amber became an accountant, which people always found difficult to believe. She did not possess the stereotypical personality of an accountant. She was an optimistic, joyful, "life of the party" cheerleader type. In fact, she had been a cheerleader all throughout high school and college. Conner would often say to Amber, "You know, your unforgettable smile is the inspiration to all of my success." This was an enormous compliment and true. With overwhelming student loans, an old 71 Imperial LeBaron, and no assistance from their families, Amber and Conner worked hard to build their own marketing business from the ground up. They started in the spare bedroom of their old apartment in the town below. Conner was a classic over achiever, and Amber was brilliant with numbers and finances. She also possessed the natural beauty of a homegrown supermodel. In addition, her smile was the inspiration for the name and logo that had become the calling card for the Conner empire: Unforgettable Inc.

Conner waved back at Amber as he continued down the driveway. He could not help but grin as the picture of her smile invaded every portal of his senses. As he reached the end of the drive, his grin began to fade. He slowed down his pace until he came to a complete stop. He stood and stared into the trees. Once the cold winter chill had pilfered the last drop of warmth from his well-insulated body, he moved. He put his head into his hands and knelt down in the snow. He began to cry; his tears froze upon his face. With deep sorrow, realizations emerged. He would never see that smile again; he would never kiss those lips; he would never hold her just to hold her. Amber was gone and she was never coming back. Nevertheless, Conner still saw her waving to him, still saw her unforgettable smile, and still heard her encouraging him to keep running. This morning there would be no running. He had tried. However, all he wanted to do was go back to the house and achieve drunken stupor status once again.

Raphael watched from the trees as Conner slowly made his way back to the house. It had been two months since Amber left the earth. Two months since Amber poured out her final words. Two months since Conner started drinking.

It's been two months since Amber placed her words in my care. And two months since...I failed, Raphael thought.

The words she used in her letter to Conner moved Raphael. Unfortunately, every attempt to deliver her letter had been unsuccessful. He left it on Conner's bed, on the nightstand, on the bathroom sink, by the TV remote, on the kitchen table. He even tried putting it in the refrigerator and in what had become the liquor cabinet. Conner never saw the envelope with his name on it; or, he chose to ignore it. His sorrow and pain had driven him to a place of depression that made it difficult for him to care about anything or anyone.

Raphael watched Conner stare at Amber's picture for hours at a time. Staring was not bad. The problem was the habit he paired with his staring. Guzzling, that was the problem: bottle after bottle of whiskey, gin, rum, cheap beer, and wine. Raphael did not know much about the consumption of alcohol, but he did not think it was good that Conner was gulping down bottle after bottle of every kind of liquor he could get his hands on.

Next to the picture of Amber was another picture, a picture that remained turned over, a picture of three children. Conner attempted to ignore this picture. In the early years of marriage, Conner and Amber stayed consumed with earning degrees and establishing the business. They did not even talk about children. Once college was complete and the business was established, Amber yearned for a child. Conner, consumed with the business, was not sure of the timing. However, his undying adoration for Amber caused him to change his mind. They began to attempt to build a family. After three years of trying and an abundance of medical testing and advice, the medical community informed them that Amber was unable to bear a child. She was heartbroken. Conner was frustrated and deeply distressed; his heart ached for Amber.

After facing the reality that she was unable to become pregnant, Amber warmed up to the idea of adopting. As she researched the possibility, she realized what an incredible gift adoption could be for the child and the parents. She researched many adoption agencies and read every story on adoption she could find. Locating a baby consumed her. On March 19 of that year, they adopted their first child, a baby boy whom they named Daniel Conner Mason. Two years later, they adopted another boy whom they named Christopher David Mason.

Amber was a wonderful mother and Conner quickly embraced fatherhood, as the boys became the center of their lives. At the same time, Unforgettable Inc. was becoming one of the most sought after marketing firms in the nation. Amber stayed as beautiful as the day he met her, and the boys made her smile seem to shine even brighter. Conner was feeling on top of the world and very blessed with his God-given family.

One day, when Daniel was nine and Christopher was seven, existence at the Mason household changed. It is a day that Conner will never forget. He worked late that day but was anxious to get home. Amber left work early, picked up the boys from school and rushed back to the house to make dinner. She called Conner to confirm he would be home by six. He told her he would try. He pulled into the driveway at 6:45 p.m. Amber met him at the door and greeted him with her radiant smile. She pulled him close, placed that unforgettable mouth on his, and kissed him as if her life depended on it.

"What is this all about?" he inquired with a grin.

"What, can't a wife passionately kiss her husband when he's late for dinner?" she replied as she playfully tilted her head and smiled.

Now Conner was a little confused, "Yeah...I guess I was expecting a smack from the frying pan, not a smack from your pretty little mouth!"

He pulled her close and kissed her again, enjoying the moment.

The boys watched from the living room, gave each other looks of disgust, and then yelled out together, "UGH...that's gross, Dad!"

Conner yelled back, "Oh yeah!"

He ran in and tackled both of them as they started a wrestling-tickling match. Amber laughed as she watched from the kitchen. Joy filled the house as she called them into the dining room for dinner. They sat to eat and enjoyed small talk of the boys' day at school and talk of their sporting tryouts. Conner shared good news of another major client he signed with Unforgettable Inc. Amber listened intently, enjoying the manly exploits of all three of her boys.

Conner noticed she was not talking and turned to ask, "What about you, babe...what's going on with you?"

Her eyes twinkled as if she had been waiting for him to ask the question. She turned toward him, and he stared intently into her eyes. Her smile conveyed a joy that words could not express.

"Are you...?" Conner asked.

"Yes..." she said, "I am pregnant!"

The boys yelled out, "What...pregnant?"

"I can't believe it, I thought it was impossible! I mean, the doctors said..." Conner breathed out every word. "Are you sure?"

"Yes...It's true! I went to the doctor today. I didn't tell you because I wanted to be certain before I said anything...please don't be mad!"

"Mad? Are you kidding? This is wonderful! This is a miracle child!"

Conner jumped up from the table and picked Amber up in his arms. He hugged her and kissed her cheek as he swung her around in the air.

"Uh, honey..." Amber spoke up, "I'm pregnant; you may want to be a little more careful."

"Oh yeah...sorry. I just cannot believe this. This is amazing!"

Christopher said, "Does this mean that I won't be the youngest anymore?"

"Oh man...what if it's a girl!" Daniel blurted.

Conner pulled Amber and the boys together for a group hug. "Listen, everything is going to be just fine. Boy, girl...it does not matter. We will just have one more in the Mason Clan to love!"

Almost seven and a half months later, the new little Mason edition arrived. Conner announced, "We will call her Amber Grace. Amber after her amazing mother and Grace because it's a miracle she is here."

It appeared the Masons had the perfect lives. Three beautiful children (one of which, according to the medical experts, should not have existed), a thriving business, and a love for each other that seemed to grow by the moment. It was a season of joy. A season Conner thought would last forever. It lasted for almost three years; then came "the news."

CHAPTER 13

"What?" Conner gasped. "How can this be?" He yelled at his cell phone.

He abruptly ended the conversation, grabbed his keys, and ran to his car. His mind filled with questions. His emotions fluctuated from moment to moment. Fear, confusion, hope, desperation, love, despair, panic, and faith all seemed to be engaged in a no holds barred death match. Panic and fear appeared to be the odds on favorites to win.

Cancer...the word weighed a ton. The word demanded prominence at the center stage of his mind.

Cancer. Why? How? She was sick for six months and not one doctor could figure out what was wrong; and now, after all this time, just now we find out it's cancer all along? The thought infuriated Conner. *Not just cancer...inoperable cancer! What was the word the doctor used...terminal? Yeah, that's it...terminal cancer!* His thoughts propelled his senses into the next round of Emotional Death Match.

Conner pulled into the hospital parking lot focused on one thing: Amber. The crash of his car into the unmanned ambulance propelled him back into reality. The airbag deployed and threw him back against his seat. He felt the blood dripping down his forehead. Tapping...he heard tapping. Someone was at his window.

I have to get out, he thought. *Seatbelt, undo my seatbelt.*

He reached down and attempted to release himself. The door opened and two paramedics began to pull him out of the car.

He heard them talking, "Grab his arms! Now gently turn his body...that's it! Steady...Ok... we got him."

Conner felt himself moving. He was rolling. "Am I on a stretcher? Where are we going?"

Blaine, one of the paramedics consoled him, "Just relax, sir, everything is going to be okay."

Conner fought to get up, "But...let me go...I have to get to her...AMBER!"

Marco, the other paramedic held Conner down and smiled, "No worries, Conner...no worries!"

Conner looked up, "How do you know my name?"

Marco just smiled. Conner passed out as they rolled him into the emergency room.

"Good morning, sweetheart!"

Conner thought it was the voice of an angel. It was. He turned over in his hospital bed searching for the owner of the voice. He rubbed his eyes. He smiled as Amber's face came into focus. There she was, in her cute little hospital gown: his angel. He stared. He always stared when he saw her. He could not help himself.

There it is, he thought. *The most unforgettable smile in the world.*

Every tooth in her mouth was on display as she grinned.

"How's my boy?" she said.

"I'm not worried about me...how are you?" Conner asked.

"Aww...I'm great! Just look at me!" She twirled around, showing off her new hospital issued attire.

Conner had to admit. She looked great, as cute as ever. She even made that hospital gown look good. However, the word was still there—the heavy word. The word he did not want to speak: *Cancer.*

He did not want to ask, she looked so happy. Nevertheless, he had to know, "Amber, what are the doctors saying?"

Her smile shrunk. She sighed as she looked down.

Then her big grin appeared again as she crawled into the hospital bed with him, "Let's not worry about what the doctors have to say! Let's just enjoy the fact that we both look so good in these hospital gowns!" She put her arm around him and then playfully said, "Well at least I do!"

Conner laughed. He held her and wondered what he did to deserve this incredible woman beside him.

As he held her close, he hid the tears. A nurse came in to check on Conner. She began to say something. Dr. Lamure interrupted her. He had a chart in his hands that read, "Amber Mason."

"Uh, why don't we leave them alone for now?" he said.

The nurse smiled and nodded as she closed the door and walked away.

Conner and Amber talked for hours as they held each other. They laughed as they discussed their boys and little Amber Grace who were currently in the care of Conner's mother. They talked about first dates and kisses, late nights with no money, their home, favorite movies, embarrassing moments, their old car, romantic get-a-ways, and family members—good and bad. They even talked about dreams for the future. However, they did not discuss that word. It was too heavy for this moment.

Knock, Knock.

Dr. Lamure knocked on the door. Conner ignored it. He did not want the moment to end. He wanted to hold Amber forever. He wanted to wake up in their house with her in his arms and three children jumping on their bed. He wanted to stare at her smile and never look away. He wanted to make her coffee, wipe her tears, walk in the mountains with her, throw snowballs, let her have the remote, and take her to her favorite restaurant. He wanted to...

"Hello, Amber. Hello, Mr. Mason, I am Dr. Lamure. We need to talk."

There have been great advancements in the fight against cancer, and Conner Mason may know them all. He spared no expense in Amber's fight. Moreover, prayer became his conversation of choice, for praying was all he did. Ten months after his first meeting with Dr. Lamure, he was at Amber's bed side listening to another doctor tell him, "I'm sorry. We have done all that we can. There is nothing more we can do." He had grown used to those words. He was numb to them.

He held Amber's hand as he had many times before. Through radiation, chemo, vitamins, special juices, and every medical and holistic treatment known to man, he was there—holding her hand. It had been a long ten months. It felt like a lifetime.

Through all of this time, Amber never lost hope; she never lost faith. She was a fighter. Conner stared at her as he had done a million times before. Even with her hair gone, face puffy, and tubing coming out from all over, he could not stop staring at her.

He leaned down to kiss her and said, "You are the most beautiful woman that has ever lived, and I have never thought you were more beautiful than now."

As he spoke the words, Amber opened her eyes and with what little strength she had left...she smiled.

Conner held her close as she went back to sleep. Then he knelt beside her bed. Since the first day with Dr. Lamure, he had prayed every day for her to be well. Now, as he listened to her fighting for breath and growing weaker by the day, he prayed a different prayer: an honest prayer.

"God...I don't know what to ask for anymore. I just want her well; I just want her back...totally. But I cannot stand to see her like this anymore. So...if she would be better with you, if she could be totally well where you are, then please...take her home." He started weeping as he cried out the last words, "I just want what's best for her! Don't let her suffer anymore...please."

He reached up and held her hand.

She opened her eyes and whispered, "Conner, I love you."

Her smile fought to appear one more time.

He stared at her as he always did, "I love you, too!"

He continued to hold her hand as they both fell asleep. She did not wake up.

Raphael was about to give up on this assignment. He had never failed; but he was losing hope. Two months was a long time.

His thoughts revealed his frustration; *maybe I should grab him and shake him, then hold him down as I read him the letter. I do not think the Commander would like that too much, but it might get the job done!*

Something interrupted his thoughts. Conner was on his knees, praying.

"God...where are You in all of this? Are You still here? Please...I need to know that I am going to be all right. I feel like I'm losing my mind."

"Now's my chance," Raphael whispered.

He had placed Amber's letter everywhere. Now, he was going to make the placement more than obvious. Conner, rolled up on the floor with his head in his hands, continuing to cry and pray. Raphael did his best stealth bomber impersonation and soared over the top of Conner's head.

No ignoring this, Raphael thought.

Conner felt something hit his head. Even in his frenzied state of mind, the corner of the envelope stung like a needle. Raphael smiled as Conner looked to see what hit him.

"I dropped the letter" is what Raphael would write on the official report. He smiled as he thought, *'I pushed it with force' would be more honest, or maybe 'I threw it with all of my might' would be more accurate.*

Regardless of what he stated on the "official report," he was certain of one thing: he had finally succeeded in the delivery.

Conner rubbed the back of his head then picked up the envelope now lying in front of him. He wore a puzzled look as he examined the mysterious object.

"Where did this...?" He looked up.

Then something on the envelope caught his attention: CONNER MASON. *That's me,* he thought.

His confusion melted into curiosity. Unwinding like a slow motion replay at a football game, he opened the envelope.

He fell back against his recliner and began to read.

Dear Sweet Conner,

No matter how I try to understand, I can't; and I'm sure there are no words to describe the confusion you must be experiencing. But please know...I am at total peace and nothing hurts! No more treatments! No more radiation! No more diagnosis! Hey...God answered our prayers, I am cancer free!

Sure not the way we planned it, but Conner, it's okay. I have been embraced by a peace that I never knew was possible. I am surrounded by the love of God. Completely. I don't know how to explain this! Just know, besides you, it is the best thing I have ever experienced.

Conner, this letter is coming to you because I've been allowed to share my final words with you. Don't ask me how. Just be grateful, I know I am! I am deeply sorry for your pain, your loss. I would do anything to take it away. I know you miss me; I miss you, too. It is strange though...I don't think time works here as it does there. I have a sense that we will reunite shortly. Do you remember how we used to talk about how great it will be to spend eternity in Heaven, to meet Jesus, to experience life forever in His presence, no more pain, no more tears? Well, it is better than we thought! And as much as you looked forward to being here before, well now it will be even better—because I am here!

Though our lives on earth are temporary, they are still a gift. Everyday our lives are full of gifts; and there was no greater gift in my life than you. I always knew how much God loved me because He sent me you. I cannot imagine any other man that I would have wanted to spend my life with. You were definitely a "cut above" in the Husband department. You worked hard but always had time for the children and me. I never grew tired of getting lost in your big brown eyes or melting away in your embrace. Even when we fought, I would be secretly excited just thinking about making up. You are everything a woman could dream of in a husband. I know these memories may bring pain because now they represent loss. But that will pass and the day will come when all you will do when you think of me is smile.

Conner, you were the love of my life and I know my leaving is painful. Though you miss me, don't worry about me. As I have said, I am in a wonderful place, and someday...you will join me. But that day is not now. And I want to talk to you about...now.

Conner, you always listened to me; always valued my opinion. So, I am asking you to please, listen to me one more time. I know you do not want to hear these words, but you must.

Conner Mason...you must go on.

You must go on—not just for you—but also for our kids. As much as I needed you, now there are three beautiful children who need their father. I am sure they don't understand why their mother is gone. And the worst thing for them would be to also lose their father. Conner, you are a man that knows how to love, that knows how to give of himself. You know how to sacrifice. You know how to creatively teach life lessons; you know how to turn chores into a fun family game; you know how to impart the stuff of life that matters. So...please! Get up and be the father our children need you to be! Love them, hold them, cry with them, laugh with them, and lead them. Right now, they need to be your purpose: the reason you get up. Let them know that I am in a wonderful place; that I am with God; that I am not hurting; that I am smiling; and that they will see me again.

Conner, you will always share a bond of love with them; you will always share the memories of me no one else can. But please, don't just share memories of a life that was; help them live a life that is. Help them live...NOW!

Now is the time to let them know that you love them, that you need them and that the four of you will continue to be a family. I know I was always cautious about what the kids ate and what they did, but I give you permission now to spoil them a little...just a little!

As much as you were my everything, as much as you were my strength, as much as you were my life, now that must change. Now, I will be waiting: waiting for you, waiting for the kids. However, as I said, time is different here, so I won't be waiting long. Live your life. Be the man I know you are. Be the father our kids need you to be. Live every moment as the gift it is.

And me...I'll see you in a little while!

Big smiles! I love you,

Amber

Conner was overwhelmed. He held the letter to his chest and cried out, "Amber! Oh God, how I love you! Amber...I am sorry! I am so sorry! I have neglected our kids. What have I done? I didn't mean to. I just love you so much. I miss you more than I can bear. I don't know how...I don't know how to go on!"

Raphael watched as Conner looked up. His words now seemed directed to the Commander.

"Oh God! Help me! Please God...help me!"

Now that's a prayer, Raphael thought, *simple, real, and from the heart.*

He knew the Commander was listening and he could sense His presence once again. There was always such peace when He was around. Conner must have felt it.

His crying subsided, and he lifted up his head as he continued, "Listen, God, as much as it hurts...I have to get up! I have to get my kids; I have to be a father. Please help me! Help me in this pain. And help me with my kids; I hope they can forgive me!"

Once again, he began to cry.

Raphael continued to watch hidden in the shadows of the unlit living room. Conner stood up and moved toward the phone. He stared ahead as he picked it up and began to dial. He closed his eyes. The phone rang three times before someone answered it. It was his mother on the other end.

"Mom?" Pause. "Yeah it's me. Are the kids ok?"

Raphael smiled as he listened to the one-sided conversation. He knew Conner was still hurting and would be for some time. Nevertheless, he was taking steps. Raphael did not totally understand how human pain worked, but he had seen people become better people because of it: hard to understand. From what he observed, humans did not understand it either. The Commander did though. He understood. Not only did He understand, He somehow used the pain to help people grow. Raphael observed how some people who had experienced the greatest pain then led some of the most extraordinary lives. Some became more compassionate and understanding. Some became more motivated to do things that touched the lives of others. Some became fervent about completing lifelong dreams. It appeared that those who reached out to the Commander became the ones who changed for the better.

Raphael listened in again on Conner's conversation, "Mom...tell the kids I love them. And...tell them to get packed. Daddy is coming to get them. Yeah. That's right. I will be there in two hours. What? Yes mom, I am going to be ok. I love you too."

CHAPTER 14

Landon stared at the door as a loud knock interrupted this otherwise peaceful occasion.

"Open up!" the voice demanded.

Then…more knocking. He leaned back in his chair and took another sip of his bourbon and water. He did not intend to open the door. He did not know exactly who was on the other side, but he knew they had a gun or guns. He had been waiting for them.

Why rush the inevitable? he thought. He never intended for his life to end like this; yet, here he was.

As he reflected on how he ended up here, a coercing vision stormed onto center stage of his thoughts. The memory was powerful. He reached into his pocket and pulled out his wallet. He found an old, weathered photo and held it close to his chest.

"Ariel…my dear, sweet girl, I am so sorry."

Landon Michaels was a powerful man: wealthy, ruthless, and prosperous in business. He made a decision at a young age that he was going to succeed no matter what the cost. Unfortunately, his relentless pursuit to build his empire produced many enemies along the way. He had always been able to pay his way out of any mess he created. However, this time, he had made the wrong people mad. There was no amount of money that could stop the fact his life was about to end. Nevertheless, even in the midst of his own demise, dying was not his greatest regret. His greatest regret was that he had not been a part of his daughter's life.

Landon married young and divorced soon after. He always took care of his ex-wife—Lisa, even though she never wanted their daughter to know him. Lisa knew the type of people Landon associated with, and she did not want Ariel propelled into the dangerous world of payoffs, mafia ties, and self-advancement at any price. In addition, Lisa was concerned that Landon's associates might discover he had a daughter. That knowledge would put Ariel at danger for the rest of her life.

Landon and Lisa came to a mutual agreement concerning Ariel: she would never know him and all legal documents proving him as her father would stay hidden…forever.

This did not stop Landon from observing Ariel from a distance. Wealth and power had its privileges. For Landon, employing a private investigator to keep an eye on his daughter was one of them.

He never attended one of her school functions or sporting events. Yet, he had files full of pictures, transcripts, SAT scores, track results, and various other details such as her first kiss, first job application, and a complete FBI background check on her senior prom date (stuff any dad would want to know). He knew her mother would not approve, but it was the only way he felt he could stay a part of Ariel's life.

Often, when Ariel was in need of the finances to pay for something she really wanted, money would appear in her savings account. The first time it happened, she was shocked and immediately told her mother. Her mom made her report it to the bank and the money was returned to sender. The next time this "banking error" occurred, Ariel just smiled and withdrew the money. She wondered where it came from, but she never told her mom again.

Landon stared at the old, worn-out picture. His investigator provided him with many photos of Ariel, but the one he was now holding was still his favorite. It was the last thing Lisa gave him. When Ariel was five years old, Landon called Lisa and asked for a meeting. She reluctantly agreed and made sure he understood this would be their last reunion. They met in an old diner on the other side of town. It was in a neighborhood Landon knew well—his kind of people. Lisa hated that part of town and avoided even driving through, much less stopping.

The pounding on his door intensified. He closed his eyes and leaned back in his chair. He blocked out the noise by rehearsing his last conversation with Lisa word for word. Landon remembered every moment of that final meeting.

He was sitting in the corner booth of the diner as she walked in.

How in the world did I ever let her go? he thought.

She approached without saying a word and sat down with her legs still in the aisle; she was not planning on staying.

"Wow Lisa, you look beautiful!" Landon stood up and attempted to hug her.

She stiffened and leaned back not wanting to relinquish even the slightest hint of affection.

"Hello, Landon…what do you want?"

"Hey, why don't we eat while we're here? And catch up on old times!"

"Is that why you asked me here? To catch up?" She hesitated with a look of disbelief, "Landon, there is nothing about you that I want to catch up with."

Landon looked at her and presented his famous pout complete with puppy dog eyes and downturned lips. There was a time when this would have worked on Lisa; in fact, as she recollected, it was because of this very look Ariel came to be.

"Oh no Landon! Really? The pout? That may have worked on the naïve little eighteen-year old I used to be, but Lisa has grown up."

"I just thought…"

"I don't care what you thought! If you asked me here as some lame attempt to reignite an old flame, well you have wasted both of our time! Because there is nothing to ignite. Not one spark."

"Hey, c'mon now. Let's just eat and talk. We can discuss anything you want. I'm just happy to see you; I don't want anything but to share a meal with an old friend."

"Seriously? Landon, I've never known you to do anything that wasn't calculated, conniving, and selfishly motivated. Now c'mon… what is this really all about? Why did you want to see me?"

"Oh Lisa, Lisa, Lisa…You know me too well; and you're right about me. All of it. I am selfish and conniving and everything you said."

"Well, it's good that you can admit it. That's the first step toward change."

"Marry me!"

"What?"

"Marry me. C'mon, Lisa. We're perfect for each other! And yes I am selfish and a liar and a lot of bad things, but Lisa...you are the one person that I cannot get away with being like that. You make me honest. I need you! I know it didn't work out the first time, but this time it will be different."

Lisa was speechless. She stared at Landon with an "is this really happening" type of stare.

Landon continued, "Listen, you don't have to decide right now, but think about it. We can take it real slow. Please, let's just give us another chance. I will do whatever you want, I'll change...trust me."

"Trust you! Are you serious? Trust you? Do you remember what happened the last time you told me to trust you? Do you want the play-by-play? Let's see...you were supposed to be watching Ariel—our daughter—who was only one year old at the time. Is this ringing a bell? Ariel had just learned to walk and had escaped from her crib and was about to topple down the staircase. Fortunately, I came home just in time to catch her as she was falling to her death! Unfortunately, I also came back just in time to hear you... in the bedroom...giving Mariana, the Spanish maid, an English lesson. At least I assume that's what you were doing, because she sure knew how to yell your name!"

Landon just stared at her.

"Listen, I'm done here." Lisa stood up, grabbed her purse, and began to leave.

"Wait please!"

Lisa stopped. She rolled her eyes and pinched her lips together. She slowly turned and stared at Landon without speaking.

"Ok, so we can't work things out. Alright, I just thought it was worth a try."

"Landon, you have thirty seconds to tell me what you want, before you see me walk away for the last time."

"Let me see her."

"What?"

"Let me see Ariel."

"Alright, that's it. This conversation is over, because you are crazy!"

"Just once. You don't even have to tell her I'm her dad. Just have me over as a friend and let us share a meal together."

"Landon," Lisa shook her head and closed her eyes. She searched for words, but the right ones escaped her.

"Lisa, just one time. Then I will leave you and her alone forever. C'mon, you owe me this."

Suddenly, Lisa had no trouble finding the words to say, "What? I owe you! Why? Because you have given me money? What about the fact that you ruined my life? What about the fact that I am in fear every day that some of your 'associates' will discover you have a daughter and will kidnap her or something worse? I owe you? The only reason I even tolerate you is because you gave me Ariel. But you will never see her again! Do you understand me! Never!"

Lisa turned to leave as everyone in the diner stared in stunned silence. She stopped midway to the door and walked back.

"You really want to see her? Fine, here." She reached into her purse and took out a recent photo of Ariel. Take this, and leave us alone!"

She threw it down and walked away.

Landon took hold of the photo and held it up. The memory was over. The knocking on the door ended. Two armed men broke down the door and stepped through.

The biggest one spoke, "Are you Landon Michaels?"

He nodded.

The two men opened fire. He held the photo to his heart as multiple bullets ripped through his body.

Behind the curtain, Raphael held his hands over his eyes. This was difficult to watch, even for an angel.

CHAPTER 15

"Where is my book bag?" Ariel exclaimed as she rearranged her already messy room. "Oh, there it is." She picked it up and threw in her unfinished history homework. "Where's my mother? Doesn't she know I'm going to be late?" Just as she spoke the words, her mother pulled up.

Ariel ran downstairs as her mother—Lisa—came through the front door.

"Why are you all dressed in black?" Ariel asked.

Lisa hesitated before she answered. "Oh, just had to say good-bye to an old friend."

"Did they die?"

"Yes dear, I was at a funeral. But don't worry, it was no one you knew or would want to know."

"Well, are you sad?"

Lisa paused. Honestly, she was sad; but she would never admit it to herself.

"Sure I'm sad, honey. A little, but…life goes on."

"So you weren't real close?"

"No Ariel, we weren't real close. Anyways, why all the questions? Don't you have a study group to get to?"

"Yes! And I'm late, because I've been waiting for you!"

Lisa smiled. Thoughts of the "friend" who passed captured her attention. *Did I do the right thing by keeping him out of Ariel's life? Should I have given him another chance? Am I crazy? Surely, I did the right thing. I mean, he was a criminal, wasn't he? Or were just his friends the bad guys? Maybe I could have ignored that part of his life. Should I tell Ariel? Is it fair that she never knew her own father? Now she never will, and...that's my fault!*

"Mom! C'mon! What's up with you? You are just staring at the wall! What are you thinking about anyways?"

"Oh, nothing. Just...nothing."

"Well I think it's something. But right now we have to leave. Remember, me...study group...history! Do you want me to fail out of my senior year and not go to college? Come on!"

"You're right. I am sorry Ariel. Just lost in my thoughts. Get your stuff and let's go."

Rules. Raphael was thinking about them again. He was mulling over the many rules and guidelines he was required to follow. Of course, he had broken a few. Nevertheless, he did want to do things correctly and, most of all, he wanted to please the Commander. Especially after his recent meeting with Him.

For Raphael, the meeting was incredible and something he could not describe in words. The face-to-face encounter renewed his desire to please Him. The Commander had that kind of effect.

With his renewed sense of purpose, a particular guideline captivated Raphael's mind: *When an unwritten letter is delivered, it can only be read by the first person who finds it.* Now, in all of his time delivering letters, he never had one picked up by the wrong person. Not one. He was proud of that record. He understood why the Commander had set up this guideline. It could be confusing for someone to read a letter intended for someone else. In addition, there was often the revealing of very private feelings, emotions, and thoughts intended specifically for the targeted recipient.

Lisa—Ariel's overprotective, nosy mother was the reason Raphael found himself thinking about this particular rule. She often went into Ariel's room and went through her stuff. Lisa justified her actions by saying she was just being cautious. This came from the fear she always had of Landon attempting to contact Ariel and secretly meet with her.

Raphael thought about how mad Lisa would be if she knew Landon anonymously gave Ariel money and hired a private investigator to document her entire life. The thought amused him. *Now, where can I put this letter where her mother won't find it?*

Raphael was not surprised when Landon chose to leave his unwritten letter with Ariel. He expected it. He was somewhat surprised about some of the content though. He had always made sure the letters delivered met with the Commander's specifications: they had to communicate encouragement, comfort, or love. Normally this was not an issue, and this time was no exception. Though Ariel might experience shock, the letter was full of love and encouragement. It might also bring up some confusion and anger between Ariel and her mother. While this concerned Raphael, it was not his primary issue. What concerned him most was a type of information communicated in this letter that Raphael had never dealt with before. This was the first time he had actually contacted the office of the Commander in order to have someone else preview a letter's content. The Commander gave His okay; and, with that, Raphael was excited to make his delivery.

However, he still had a problem, "Where do I put this letter? Hey..." Raphael looked up, "I could use a little help here!" Then it came to him; he knew the perfect spot.

Ariel left her study group and began to walk down to the local coffee shop. Her mother thought her group lasted for four hours; it only lasted for two. Ariel may have given her the idea it was longer. On her way to the coffee shop, Ariel would normally stop at the bank to cash her meager paycheck. She worked a few hours a week at a local pet store; she loved animals.

As she entered the bank, Raphael was waiting. His plan was coming together. Ariel was keeping her normal schedule. Now, he needed to get behind the teller and time the placement of the letter just right. His plan was to put it in the envelope with the money Ariel received back.

As he watched the line diminish and Ariel get closer to the front he suddenly thought, *What am I doing? This is crazy!* His ideas often sounded better in the planning stage than in the execution.

He knew he would have one shot. *Ok...she's almost to the front.*

Ariel waited as the man before her finished his transaction.

She smiled and said, "Hello" as she moved to the front of the line.

Raphael—silent and invisible—stood directly behind the teller. As she greeted Ariel, Raphael quickly opened the top envelope and began to slip the letter inside. The teller turned, just as Raphael was about done. She reached for the envelope with the letter still partially sticking out.

Oh no! Raphael thought.

Fearful the teller would see the letter, he reached to pull it out. Just as he did, a noise came from over by the front of the bank. Everybody turned to see what it was. Someone had fallen and knocked over the trashcan near the door. The teller was distracted. Raphael took advantage of the moment and pushed the letter completely into the envelope.

The teller turned back around and placed the money into the envelope. In her distracted state, she did not notice the letter.

The teller smiled and handed Ariel her money as she asked, "Is there anything else I can do for you today?"

Ariel smiled and said, "No."

She thanked the teller and headed for the door.

Raphael let out a big sigh of relief.

"That was a bad idea," he said to himself. "Oh well!"

Anxious to see how Ariel was going to react, he swiftly moved to the bank exit. As he left, he saw a man picking up the garbage can and putting the trash back in.

He sure looks familiar, Raphael thought. He could not see Ariel. *I had better hurry. I don't want to miss this.*

Ariel was already at the coffee shop. Raphael flew in and found a place in the back. He watched as she went to the counter to make her purchase. As she reached into her bank envelope, something slipped out. She reached down to pick it up.

That's strange, she thought. *What is this? It has my name on it.*

Ariel handed over her money to pay for her "double espresso, two percent, extra foam with a hint of cinnamon" caramel latte. She was holding the mysterious piece of paper with her name on it as she waited. She began to open it when the clerk behind the counter handed over her drink. Raphael watched in anticipation as she made her way to a table in the back. *Girl, you're about to get the biggest piece of news of your life; well, several pieces!*

She sat down her latte and opened up the paper she was holding. The next time that latte would be touched would be when someone was throwing it in the garbage, because Ariel never took another sip. Raphael watched as she read the first line of her mysterious piece of paper:

Dear Ariel,

I do not even know how to begin. Well, maybe I should start with an introduction. Hi, my name is Landon Michaels. I am your father.

Ariel did not wait for her mom to pick her up. Instead, she rode a bus to her side of town, and then ran the rest of the way home. She texted her mother and told her that the study group had ended early and she had a ride.

Her mom texted, "Ok, I'll be home in a few hours."

Ariel had a little time to think about everything she had just learned. *I have a father but I will never know him. How could my mom do this? But how could she not? And then there's the other news...wow! What am I going to say to my mother?*

A lifetime worth of questions churned inside her. Memories that never were began to create themselves; visions of a father that never was but could have been. Ariel was pacing and thinking. As she walked by the kitchen table, something caught her eye: the bright yellow phone book. She opened it up and turned to churches. Normally when she was searching for something, she would just go to her laptop and Google it. However, she was caught up in the moment, and the yellow pages were right there. She quickly began to scan through addresses listed under every Catholic Church she could find. Then, she stopped. There it was; and there was the number.

Should I call now or should I wait for my mom? Probably I should wait. She pulled out her cell phone, *Maybe I'll just call. But what if everyone speaks Spanish? My mom does speak a little Spanish. Alright…I'll wait.*

As she waited for her mother to return, she pulled out the letter and read it one more time.

Dear Ariel,

I do not even know how to begin. Well, maybe I should start with an introduction. Hi, my name is Landon Michaels. I am your father.

As difficult as this may be for you to believe, this is not a joke. This is for real. My greatest regret in telling you this is that we will never have the chance to meet. As if finding out that I am your father is not enough of a shock for you, let me give you another one: I am dead. I know, how can I be writing this then? Well…you will just have to trust me on this one. I really am your father, and I really am dead and these really are my words.

I have dreamed of meeting with you a thousand times. More likely, a thousand times a day. Believe it or not, I know a lot about you. I know your name is Ariel Jewel. For the record, I picked out the Ariel part. I know you were born on June 27, on a Wednesday, at 4:15 in the morning. I also know that was the first and last time you were ever up early! I know that you do not like school, but make very good grades and you are on the honor roll. I know you want to go to college, but are concerned about how you will pay for it. I know you have had three different boyfriends in high school. I also know that only one of them was worthy of you. That was Brian by the way. I also know that when your prom date tried to get fresh, you dropped him to the ground by kicking him in his most vulnerable spot; you did this in the parking lot in front of all of his friends and half of the senior class. Way to go, girl!

I know you like nice things like leather jackets, new shoes, and certain concert tickets. I know your mother would not like the fact that I paid for all of those things for you. Yeah, I was your mysterious donor. But let's just keep that a secret.

I know that you love your mother, but sometimes the two of you have a difficult time getting along. I also know that you have always wanted to know who your father was. How I know all of these things I would rather not say, but just know this: your father loves you and has always wanted to know you.

Now you may be wondering: if I loved you and wanted to see you so bad, then why didn't I. The truth is your mother and I agreed it would be best that you and I never met. The reason why is nothing that I am proud of. You see, your dad is not what some people would consider a good person. It is not that I am a criminal; well...some people would say that I am. It is just that I made many decisions in life that hurt a lot of people. Most people would say that your dad is "ruthless in his business dealings." I would have to agree. I wanted success and I did whatever I had to do to get it. Unfortunately, that is why I am dead. I got into business with the wrong people: guys that are criminals, if you get what I mean.

You see, it is best that no one ever knows that you are my daughter. It could be dangerous to you and your mother. This brings up another matter. I know it would be real easy for you to be mad at your mom, but I want to ask you not to be. Believe me, kid, that woman loves you. If you want to know the truth...I really love her too. She's a great person, and I wish I had been a better kind of man and we could've worked things out and stayed together. I think I would have liked that.

Ariel, if you want to be mad at someone, be mad at me. Do not blame your mother. She was just doing the right thing and protecting her little girl. And as much as I wanted to see you, I always knew it was best that I stayed out of your life.

There are so many things I would have liked to have done with you; places I would have loved to have taken you. But now, well that just ain't gonna happen. There's no need for you to be sad, 'cause you never met me. And don't regret that either. Believe me; you have the best half of your parents in your mom!

Now I know you have a lotta dreams and you want to do something with yourself. You probably get that from me. But, hopefully you got enough of your mom that you don't go about pursuing your dreams like your dad did. Your mom's gotta lot of compassion and a heart to be nice to people and help them out. From what I have seen, you've got that too. Maybe you got the best of both of us. If that's the case, then you should turn out real good.

Anyways, these dreams you have. I want to do one good thing before I leave, so here it is. I can't be there for you, but I can make sure that you at least have the opportunity to do what you want with your life. You should know, your dad had a lot of money. And, even though your mom may not believe it, most of that money was earned through good old-fashioned hard work. Since the day you were born, I have been putting money away for you—anonymously. My name is in no way attached to it; neither are any of my companies or associates. My lawyer doesn't even know about it.

It is put away in a Swiss bank account in your name with a secured numerical password. Believe me, there is enough in that account that you can go to any college you want. In fact, you could go to college for the rest of your life. There is only one person who knows about this and knows the numerical password. There is a small Catholic Church on the corner of Ashton Blvd. and Third St. There is an old priest there by the name of Father Ortiz. He does not speak much English, but he knows your name and who you are. Years ago, I told him my plan. He knows if anything happens to me that he is to wait for one week. If you haven't contacted him, then he will contact you. I trust him, and so should you.

Now, you will have to tell your mom about this. I mean she is going to notice if you are suddenly a multi-millionaire. Have fun with that! I don't think you can just tell her that I talked to you. She won't believe you anyways. Do what you think is best. If your mom gives you a hard time about the money, just have her talk to Father Ortiz, I believe he will be able to set her mind at ease.

Ariel, let me leave you with these final thoughts: I had a lot of success and made a lot of money in my life; but now, none of it means a thing. Don't make my same mistakes. Live a better life than I did; be a better person than I was; and prepare yourself for eternity. This life will end before you know it. Live it well and be prepared for the next step.

You may not believe this, but I do love you.

Wishing I had been there for you,

Dad

Ariel stared at the wall until she heard her mom open the front door.

"Mom, we need to talk."

Lisa entered the kitchen and poured herself a glass of water, "What dear?"

"I know whose funeral you went to today."

"Well of course you don't. I told you, you never knew them."

"That's true."

"Why is this even important? Why would it matter?"

"Does the name Landon Michaels ring a bell?"

Raphael heard a glass break as it hit the floor. *Well, time for me to go; I think Mom and daughter need a little time alone.*

CHAPTER 16

The sun beat down on Melissa's face. She reached up to wipe the sweat from her forehead. Her other hand was hanging on to a rock; it was the only thing preventing her from pummeling to her death on the jagged terrain below. She loved climbing; she also loved living. She began to wonder if her love for climbing was going to end her love for living. Three friends came with her to the park today, but none of them possessed her same spirit of adventure. Breaking all safety rules, she ventured out on her own. Her friends were on the other side of the mountain scaling a more "living-friendly" route to the top. Melissa had opted for the side of the mountain nicknamed "Death Trap" by previous climbers. In the last ten years, two other adventurous souls lost their lives on the jagged rocks that were now directly below her. She looked down as she hung on by one hand.

"Ugh, what was I thinking?" She breathed out.

She was losing her grip with her left hand, and her right hand was grappling to hang onto anything protruding from the mountain face.

Raphael watched as Melissa reached up to grab a rock that was not there. As he looked on, waiting to make his appearance, he felt someone behind him.

As he turned, a familiar voice spoke, "Hey, Raphee!" It was Michael the archangel.

"What are you doing here?" Raphael exclaimed.

"Raphee, do you like your job?"

"Well...yeah, of course. What could be better?"

"I am glad to hear that, Raph. Because, as you know from your recent meeting with Him, the Commander likes the job you've been doing."

"Yes, sir. It was good to hear it from Him."

Raphael did not like the casual pace the conversation was taking. He kept looking back over his shoulder wondering when Melissa was going to drop.

"Raphee, do you ever want to step in and save a life before it is too late? Ha ha...what am I saying? Of course you do... you already showed us that on the JB incident. And as you know, the Commander knew that you were going to do that. He always knows. Raphee, the Commander sent me here to inform you that your job description is...well, it is expanding. You will continue to head up the "UnWritten Letters" department as you are; however, you will also take on some occasional guardian angel duties."

"Really? That's wonderful! I mean... I love what I do, but... I will do whatever the Commander wants. If saving a life is what that means then..."

Michael interrupted, "Well, how about now?"

"You mean...?" Raphael continued to look Michael in the eye as he pointed over his shoulder at Melissa.

"Yeah…now," Michael said. "Cause she's about to fall!"

Raphael turned to see Melissa slipping off the cliff. He jumped over to where she was and placed his hand out of her sight. At that very moment, her left hand let go and she began to plunge into the canyon below. In one last attempt to stop her fall, Melissa thrust her right hand up. She hoped to grab a hold of something. A rock, a branch, a vine…anything. She was more than surprised when what felt like a hand embraced her right arm and lifted her to the top of the mountain. As Raphael released her, Melissa looked at the view around her and wondered how in the world that just happened. She let out a sigh of relief as she collapsed to the ground and began to laugh.

"Oh man…no one is ever going to believe this!" Melissa said aloud, "I'm alive! I don't know how, but I'm alive!" Laughter spilled out as she walked to where her friends were now climbing. "Hey!" she yelled, "C'mon, slow pokes. I'm already at the top!"

Raphael watched with delight then floated back to where Michael was sitting.

"That was awesome!" Raphael said.

"Yeah, that was awesome, Raphee." Michael leaned back and made a giant protruding rock his chair. Raphael was leaping on the inside; his excitement mellowed as he saw the seriousness in Michael's eyes. He took a seat sensing that he was about to experience a teaching moment.

"Raphee, what you just did was incredible, wasn't it?"

Raphael paused before answering, "Well, yes, of course. It was great…not because of me, but because a life was saved!"

"Was it just because a life was saved?"

Raphael wondered if this was a rhetorical question. He stayed quiet and waited for the answer.

"I have worked for the Commander for a long, long time and I cannot say that I totally understand Him, but I trust Him. He truly has everything under control. Now to you—and I would say this to most novice angels—and humans for that matter, saving a life like you just did would be the ultimate act that anyone could be a part of. But do you know why that is?"

Raphael shrugged his shoulders. He had no desire to interrupt the journey of learning which Michael was now leading. He wanted to get to the end.

"The reason is that down in the heart of His creation, especially humans, there is a knowing that life itself is a gift. It is precious. However, let me ask you this, Raphee. Is what you did now more important than what you have been doing? Is saving a life like this more powerful than with a final letter? You have been a part of both; which one is more important?"

Raphael knew the answer, "neither"; he did not dare speak though. Michael's words were still flowing, and Raphael was drinking it all in.

"This is where most humans miss the power of living. They do not comprehend that living a simple life dedicated to serving the Commander and others is far greater than living a life dedicated to their own selfish desires. They do not realize that being a good mom or dad can save a child's life; that consistently being a person of character impacts the people around them. This can be difficult for humans to comprehend. In the midst of their numerous commitments and overwhelming requirements of life, they can lose their motivation to be parents to their kids, to be a good employee, or to be kind to a neighbor. They can lose their motivation for many things. People do not always realize the impact small everyday decisions have on those around them. Raph, what you did today was heroic, but it was no more important than what you have been doing. What you do on a daily basis is important because it is part of the Commander's plan.

When people get to know the Commander, they realize they are part of something bigger than their daily existence. They are a part of life—the Commander's greatest gift. Sometimes people feel insignificant. They think they don't count; they feel they don't matter. If they only knew that the Commander created all of this for them. From the air they breathe to the blood that keeps their bodies moving: from the trees and flowers to the planets and stars above. How could anyone feel insignificant when one looks at the miracle of creation and realizes it is created just for them? How could they not realize that life itself is a miracle?"

Raphael was smiling now. As Michael spoke of the human condition and the Commander's love for them, Raphael was overwhelmed again with the privilege it was to be a part of anything the Commander was doing.

Michael continued, "The problem is, most people do not realize He did all of this for them, and He did so much more. He has given life as a gift. He was even willing to give His life to protect that gift. They have no idea, Raphee...they have no idea."

Raphael leapt to his feet as Michael stood.

He smiled as he spoke, "Raph my friend, I sure like you."

Raphael laughed.

Michael spoke again, "Never take yourself for granted. He created you. He has given you purpose. Every assignment matters; never forget that."

Michael began to walk towards a group of trees nearby, "Listen, Raphee, we will meet again, but right now I have another appointment I need to get to."

As Michael continued to walk away, Raphael noticed two figures step out from behind the trees. They looked familiar.

"It couldn't be!" Raphael said.

"Oh yeah," Michael said, "I believe you may know these two."

Raphael could not believe it. It appeared that Michael was about to meet with Marco and Blaine—the paramedics. He had become suspicious when he saw the two of them at multiple places.

Michael could see that Raphael was confused, "Well, Raphee... you are not the only angel with an assignment that's 'classified'!"

"You mean...they are angels?"

"You got it!"

"But, what are they doing? They don't really rescue people?"

"C'mon, Raphee, don't you remember the conversation we just had? The Commander does not just send His angels to rescue people in big ways...You should know that by now! The Commander sends His angels for many reasons. Sometimes He sends them to bring comfort; to assist people in their times of hardship."

"But if they are angels, then how come I didn't know?"

"They're pretty good aren't they? Most people think they are just two paramedics doing their job. Raphee, the truth is there are many angels that pose as humans. They are performing their 'classified' assignments unbeknownst to the sea of humanity around them. Many people have met angels and never knew."

Raphael was taking it all in, trying to understand.

"What you must remember is this…the Commander has it all under control. Everything He does has a purpose. It is easy to get caught up in your own assignment and forget that what you are doing is a piece of a much bigger picture. On the other hand, it is easy to look at the big picture and think what you are doing doesn't matter. It's the same for all of us; if it matters to the Commander, it matters!"

"Hey…would you like to meet them?" Michael pointed toward Marco and Blaine.

"Sure!"

Raphael walked with Michael over to where Marco and Blaine were waiting. They smiled as he approached.

"I always thought there was something different about you two!" Raphael said. "You sure fooled me though! I never knew."

"Did you appreciate the help at the bank?" Marco asked with a laugh.

"That was you? I wondered who knocked over that trash can!"

They spent some time talking about their individual assignments and asking questions about each other. Raphael learned that Marco and Blaine always knew about him. Even though his assignment was classified, they knew because of the frequency of their contact.

"Well, guys…we will have to reschedule our meeting," Michael said to Marco and Blaine. He pointed up as he said, "I have been summoned!"

They all looked up and laughed. They shook hands and hugged.

"Keep up the good work!" Michael said to them all.

With those final words, Michael soared into the sky and disappeared into the clouds. Marco and Blaine told Raphael goodbye then flew off to their next assignment.

Raphael stood there for a moment; staring. He was reflecting on everything that had just happened. He was thinking of being a part of the Commander's plan; of grabbing a hand and saving a life. He was thinking of how important his obedience to the Commander was in the lives of others. He was thinking of how he wished all humans would realize how much the Commander loved them, how much He did for them, and the price He paid for them.

Raphael looked up as he spoke, "Commander, it is an honor to serve You."

Somewhere up above the clouds, the Commander smiled.

CHAPTER 17

Nadia slipped on her gear and reached for her helmet.

Captain Franks yelled, "Let's go, ladies!"

He glanced at Nadia with a "no offense" look and then went back to yelling, "Looks like we got us a five alarm blaze ripping up the east side. Started in a warehouse, but has already jumped the fence into a housing complex. All hands on deck. Let's move!"

Nadia found her place in the hook-and-ladder truck. She moved over to make room for "Big Mike" and "Crazy Lou"—their nicknames fit them well. Mike, besides being tall and wide, possessed a big heart. He would often invite the local neighborhood kids over to the station when he was washing the fire trucks. He would let them get wet and even let them spray him down. Lou, on the other hand, was not very good with the public; nevertheless, the man could fight fires. He was often involved in the rescue of those trapped in places other firefighters would not go. He was also in trouble with Captain Franks on a regular basis. The Captain thought he took a few too many risks.

"Hey Foxy! You ready for this?" Big Mike smiled as he smacked Nadia on the head.

Nadia said, "You know the Fox is ready, big boy!"

Mike and Lou laughed.

"Somebody's gotta take care of you 'ladies' out there!" she continued.

"Aw girl! You all right, Foxy, you all right!" Mike said with a wink.

Nadia was the first female firefighter at the South Side firehouse, better known as Billy's Brigade. (William H. Smith—"Billy"—had been the first Captain at the South Side; he had also been the first firefighter from there to lose his life.) It took a long time for Nadia to earn the respect of her company. But now, in many ways, she was just one of the guys. She had earned the nickname Foxy.

Big Mike told her once, "We call you Foxy, because you're so cunning when you fight fires."

She laughed when he said this; she knew better.

Nadia had not only earned the respect of her own company, but of many of the firefighters and citizens in the city. The newspaper printed several articles about her, and she appeared on two local talk shows. The guys of Billy's Brigade often teased her about being a celebrity, and they would razz her about fighting fire like a girl. Nevertheless, when it came to doing her job, no one could deny her dedication and skill.

As they entered the fire zone, she could see a half a dozen other companies already in place.

This is going to be a long night, she thought. *But where else would I rather be?*

The smoke from the fire was slipping through the crack under the door. Dalton shook his head as he wondered why he decided to work late tonight. He was supposed to be at a soccer awards banquet with his son. Instead, he sat trapped on the fifth floor of the Lassiter building. He stayed late to meet with another lawyer; the lawyer never showed. Everyone else from his firm went home hours ago.

He found himself in an office, surrounded by fire, with no way out. He could see all of the fire trucks below. He tried to call someone, but the phone lines were down and he had left his cell phone in his jacket. Unfortunately, his jacket was in the smoke filled coatroom at the other end of the floor. A river of creeping fire engulfed the hallway in between.

As he sat at his desk, he picked up the picture of his family. He thought about how lucky he was to have such a beautiful, dedicated wife. He had two healthy children—a boy and a girl. He had a good job; he made good money.

But…what does all of that matter now? he thought. *I am surrounded by fire, and I am probably going to die. All because I chose to have a meeting instead of going to see my son receive a trophy.*

As he stared at the picture, wondering how he was going to get out of the building alive, he heard a noise. It sounded like a voice. It sounded like a little girl.

"Oh no," he said out loud, "It couldn't be."

He jumped from his desk and ran towards the side office door. He touched the knob to see if it was hot. It was not. He turned the knob and threw open the door.

"Daddy!"

Mia, his six-year-old daughter, leapt into his arms as tears streamed down her cheeks.

"Oh Daddy! All by myself. Nobody else! The other door is all fire and smoke is out there."

Dalton held his daughter tight.

"Everything is going to be just fine, Mia. Daddy has you. We're going to be alright!" He spoke the words to assure her, not believing a single one of them.

"Mia, how did you get in here? And where is Mommy?"

She looked at him with her head down, "Well...I know Mommy said stay in the car, but I wanted to see Daddy."

"So your mother is here?"

"Well, I don't know where she is...she ran to find you."

"But...how did you get through the fire?"

"I just went in the back up the stairs where you go and when I came out the door..." She paused and looked at her dad with big tears in her eyes, "there was smoke and hot and fire and I tried to go back but..." she burst into tears and held her dad tight.

"It's ok, Mia…you are not in trouble! You are with Daddy now. We are going to be just fine." Again, he did not believe what he was saying.

He smiled at Mia as he thought, *Oh God…what have I done*?

"Help! Please, somebody help!"

Nadia turned to see a woman running right toward her.

She ran to Nadia grabbing her by the arm and continuing to run as she yelled, "Come with me…we have to save her! She is not in the car! I am afraid she went inside! C'mon!"

Nadia stopped.

The woman continued to yell and pull on her, "C'mon…we have to go…c'mon."

Nadia responded, "Ma'am, please calm down. I want to help, but you have to tell me what you are talking about."

The woman, overcome by panic, spit out her words between gasps and cries, "My girl…she's only six…in the car…now she's gone… her dad…works on the fifth floor…Lassiter building…I'm afraid she's inside…in the fire!"

The woman broke down hysterically.

"Ma'am…okay, what is your husband's name?"

"Dalton…Dalton Richards. He is a partner with Lassiter and Associates."

"Yeah, I know who he is. And you are?"

"I'm Mary...Mary Richards. Please, this is taking too long... you have to go in! You have to save her!"

"Her...your little girl?"

"Yes...yes ...Mia! Haven't you been listening! She is only six. I left her in the car to keep her safe. I didn't want her close to the fire. I drove up, saw the building burning, and ran to find my husband. They wouldn't let me in, so I went back to the car to get my phone and try to call him. But when I got back...she was gone! Oh, God... please...you have to save her! Please! This is all my fault! I shouldn't have left her!"

"Listen, Mary is it?"

"Yes."

"We are going to do everything possible to save your husband and your daughter. Now, you said your husband was on the fifth floor?"

"Yeah, that's right. The fifth floor."

"Ok, do you know his office number?"

"Yeah, he's the last office on the left. The corner office...uh... number 517."

"And you tried to call him?"

"Yes...but there was no answer!"

"Okay. Now I need you to go with my friend here," Nadia waved to a paramedic she knew well. "Mary, this is Marco. He is going to take care of you. Stay with him, and we will let you know as soon as we find your husband and daughter."

"Ok. Thank you. Please find them! Please find my Mia!"

"We'll do our best," Nadia said.

Nadia turned and ran into Big Mike and Crazy Lou. "Listen, guys, we need to..."

Big Mike interrupted, "We heard everything. Sorry, we were eavesdropping."

"Ok then, you know what we need to do. Get your gear and let's head to the corner of the building. There is a fireproof stairwell there that should lead us to the fifth floor."

She turned and began to run toward the building.

"Oh, and Lou...see if you can get the building schematic. I overheard a maintenance guy say he grabbed a copy on his way out of the building."

Lou looked at her with a look that said, "Really?"

"Yeah Lou, I know, crazy huh? Lucky for us."

She turned to face the building and then looked up, "Lord, if you are up there..."

Raphael stared down at his notebook. He dropped it flying over the city. It fell almost 10,000 feet before hitting the pavement below. This was not the first time Raphael had dropped it. However, this time, it seemed to be malfunctioning.

The notebook was quite an interesting device. Something human inventors would love to get their hands on. It looked similar to a normal, small spiral notebook, but performed like an I-pad, only better. In addition, up until this moment, Raphael thought it was indestructible.

Now, here he was, looking at his current mission; but something was wrong. With his recent job description upgrade, he knew some of his assignments would be rescues; however, the majority would remain the normal unwritten letter collection.

"Oh man…this is a problem," he said.

He stared at his current assignment. It was a double: two names. One was a rescue; one was a letter collection. They were at the same location, at the same time. One would be saved; one would not.

The drop must have jarred the device causing the most important piece of information to be lost: which one was to receive the rescue.

Raphael thought, *I need to contact headquarters, but I don't really have time.*

The best thing for him to do was to head to the assignment location and try to figure it out. He flew up and over the city buildings. He saw the fire.

"Ok, it's almost time," he said.

He soared into the Lassiter building, landing in the hallway of the fifth floor.

Nadia paced back and forth looking down at her watch, "Where are those guys?"

She left her two-way radio in the truck, so she could not call them. It was not like Mike and Lou to be late. They should have already been there.

She looked down at her watch once more and decided to go on without them.

Nadia opened the door to the back stair well. Going alone into a flaming building is not something she would normally do. However, this time...she had a feeling. Urgency—like an adrenaline-inducing drug—was coursing through her veins.

She ran up the stairs to the fifth floor. The stairway was clear of smoke. When she arrived at the top, she checked the door. It was hot, real hot. Smoke was seeping under the fireproof door. Not a good sign.

She took her axe from her side and pushed the door open as she turned away. As if waiting for someone to invite it in, the smoke quickly took the stair well hostage. Nadia pushed through only to run into an aggressive wall of fire. She jumped back toward the stairwell. The door had already closed. The fire was closing in. There was no turning back now. She turned toward the fire and ran as fast as she could right into the middle. She was praying that somewhere on the other side was a clearing. All she found was more smoke and fire.

Then she heard it. In the midst of her breathing and the sound of her own heartbeat, somewhere over the crackling song of the fire...she heard a voice. Faint. Nevertheless, it was there. She turned toward the voice and saw a window. Two silhouettes vaguely appeared through the smoke. She ran toward them.

A man and a child...Oh God, help me help them!

The fire engulfed the room that held them. The little girl screamed. The man's eyes revealed his desperation. He held the little girl close in an attempt to protect her. Nadia felt helpless.

Even if she was able to break in, there was nowhere to take them.

"What's that?" she said.

Nadia saw a bright light glowing. It was brighter than the fire. It pierced through the smoke. As she stared at the light, she saw what it was illuminating. What she was looking at was impossible. Yet, there it was—one room in the midst of the smoke completely untouched by the fire.

She turned back toward the office window and motioned for the man and the little girl to step back. There was not much space for them between the wall and the fire. He did his best to move them out of the way.

Nadia raised her axe high into the air and swung at the window. The axe bounced off. She pulled back and tried again. Once more, she was unable to break through. She took a deep breath and gave it one more attempt. This time her axe swung with more velocity and power. It felt like someone else was swinging it for her.

Raphael smiled and pulled his hand off the axe as he watched the glass shatter. Nadia jumped through the opening and did her best to cover up the man and little girl. She assisted them into the hallway as they walked toward the one room on the fifth floor, which inexplicably repelled fire and smoke. As they walked, Nadia watched the fire and smoke part in front of them as if someone was pushing it aside.

Strange, she thought. *I have never seen anything like this.*

As soon as they entered the room and shut the door, the smoke and fire took over the hallway once again. Nadia removed her helmet and oxygen mask.

"Whew...that was close!" she said.

Now the man spoke, "No...that wasn't close...that was miraculous! How did we not die? I mean...the fire just...moved!"

"Well I'm just glad we're ok." Nadia turned toward the little girl, "Hey honey...what's your name?"

"Mia."

"That's beautiful! And...who's this guy with you?"

"That's my dad. He works here."

"Oh," Nadia turned and looked at the man, "And what's his name?"

"I'm Dalton. Dalton Richards."

"The attorney?"

"Yeah, you've heard of me?"

Nadia laughed. "Yeah, I've heard of you." She smiled as she stared at him. "I guess you don't recognize me in all my gear and smoke based make-up."

"Do we know each other?"

"I'm Nadia. Nadia Dumont. You represented my husband in our divorce proceedings three years ago."

"Oh my gosh...Nadia. Yeah, you're right. I didn't recognize you."

"Well...hello, it's me!" she said.

"Oh dear...I feel terrible. I did not treat you so well, did I? And now, here you are saving my life, and more importantly... saving my little Mia. Wow, I don't know what to say."

"Well, you don't have to say anything." Nadia smiled again as she spoke, "As for me saving you and your girl, let's wait on the thanks. We are not out of here, yet. As far as you go, I know you were just doing your job. Although, I must say...you did your job well. Didn't leave me with much!"

"I am so sorry." Dalton hung his head. "I don't know if it makes any difference, but your husband was the last client I represented in a divorce case."

"I guess after you took me for everything I owned you didn't have to work for awhile, huh?"

"Ouch...I guess I deserved that," Dalton said.

"Nadia, Foxy...you out there?"

"That sounds like my radio!" Nadia shouted, "Where did that come from?"

Mia walked to the corner of the room and picked up a two-way radio sitting underneath a chair. "Here it is!" she exclaimed. "This what you lookin' for?"

Nadia ran over and grabbed the radio, "Thank you, Mia." Nadia stared at it. "How is this possible? I left this in the truck. What is going on here?"

A familiar voice come booming over the airwaves, "Foxy...come on girl. Where you at? C'mon. Talk to Big Mike!"

Nadia pressed down the talk button, "Big Mike! Foxy's right here. Come and get me!" Tears of joy streaked down creating unique designs in the ash on her face.

"Where you been? We came to meet you, and you was already gone. We all worried about you and Captain Frank's madder than a bee in a rain storm!"

"I'm sorry, Mike; I will tell you what happened later. But listen, I have two civilians with me. I found the little girl and her dad. We are trapped in a room on the fifth floor. Looks like a conference room. I believe we are on the northwest side of the building. Did Lou get the building schematic?"

"Yeah, Foxy…we looking at it right now. I think I see the room you're in. We gonna pull the hook and ladder round to that side and come and get ya'll out."

Dalton let out a "Yes!" He pulled Mia into his lap and held her tight, "Did you hear that Mia? Nadia's firemen friends are coming to get us!"

Mia grinned as she hugged her dad.

Nadia smiled, paced, and did continuous fist pumps as she continued to talk to Big Mike, "Ok, Mike…that's great! Oh man, wait 'till I tell you everything that happened. You are not going to believe this."

"Ok, we are moving into position right now. Is there a window you can open in that room?"

Nadia looked over the wall of windows. They were sealed, fireproof, shatterproof, and top of the line, high-energy windows: great for energy efficiency, but not good when you want to get out.

She ran down the entire wall: not a single window that opened.

"Sorry, Mike. It looks like you are going to have to break through."

"Alright, you all stay over on the other side of the room."

"No problem."

Nadia made sure Dalton and Mia were away from the wall of windows. She looked around the room again and noticed a door she had not seen before. She walked over and opened it up.

"Wow…check this out," she exclaimed.

Dalton and Mia walked over to see what Nadia had discovered. They stepped through the door into a private penthouse.

"This is cool," Mia said.

"I never knew this was here," Dalton exclaimed, "Must be the company president's private room."

The hidden penthouse was well equipped with a bed, a kitchenette, a private bathroom, and a big window—that opened.

Nadia noticed it and ran back into the other room to get her radio. She saw that Mike and her crew had already made their way to the northwest side of the building. Mike was on the ladder as Lou was extending it out.

Nadia picked up the radio, "Mike…you there? I see you on the ladder. Pick up!"

She watched Mike take his radio out of his pocket, "What you want, Foxy? We not moving quick enough for you?" he said with a laugh.

"Slight change of plan. I found a big window that opens in the room right next door. I am going to open it up. You'll see me waving."

"Well, I already see someone waving...looks like your little girl."

"What?"

Nadia ran back into the penthouse to find Mia waving and yelling out the window, "Hey...we're right here! Come get us, Big Mike!"

Nadia laughed. Then she said, "Step back from there, Mia! Let's let Mike get up here and then you can step out."

She turned to Dalton, "Listen, it is only safe for Mike to take one of us at a time. So, let's send Mia first. Then you can go, and I'll go last."

"Ok...you're the professional," Dalton said.

Nadia looked back toward the window. There was Big Mike. She was never so glad to see him.

"Hey, fancy meeting you here. You come here often?" Nadia said.

"Aw Foxy, you something else. We in the middle of trying to fight a fire and you're trying to pick me up!" Big Mike laughed, "Don't you have a better line than that?"

"Mike...I'm just glad to see you. Now, get me out of here and I will buy you dinner!"

"You got it, girl." He turned toward Mia, "Who do we have here?"

"I'm Mia. And you're Big Mike aren't you?"

Mike laughed again, "You got that right! Now listen, I want you to let Nadia help you out the window and into my arms. You gotta trust big Mike, okay? I'm not gonna drop you."

"Okay."

Nadia lifted Mia up and handed her through the window into Mike's big arms.

"There you go," Nadia said, "You are safe now. Mike will take you down, and then he will come back and get your dad."

"Alright," Mia said with a smile, "Thank you, Foxy!"

Big Mike and Nadia both laughed.

Nadia stepped away from the window.

Dalton let out a sigh, "Listen, I really am sorry about the whole divorce thing."

"Aw c'mon, Mr. Richards, let it go. On a day like today, it's just good to be alive, isn't it?"

"Yeah, I guess so."

Raphael stepped out of the corner of the room. He looked down at his notebook. It was time.

CHAPTER 18

From the trees, Raphael observed the parade of cars enter the cemetery. He wondered why it always seemed cold, dark, and rainy on these days. It was a question he wanted to ask the Commander someday. He watched as people began to exit their cars and walk toward the gravesite. He was looking for her.

"There she is," he whispered.

He stood motionless as he stared at the little figure all dressed in black, holding her mother's hand—Mia.

Raphael began to think back to the day of the fire. He never knew when the moment came who he was to rescue. No word ever came down from headquarters. No direction appeared in his notebook. The decision had been his: a decision that would affect the lives of many. In the heat of the moment, he struggled. Nevertheless, a decision had to be made; and as always, the Commander had been in complete control.

As he stared at little Mia, he knew he had made the right decision. It still did not make this moment any easier. He watched for a moment longer, and then pulled an envelope out of his pocket.

"Time to make a delivery," he whispered.

He took one last look at Mia before he flew away.

"Will it ever stop raining?" Mia said as she and her mother ran up to their house.

Mary fumbled for her keys.

"Hurry, Mom…I'm getting all wet."

Mary opened the door and the two leapt out of the storm. Mia shook off the rain then hung up her coat. Mary made her way into the kitchen and put on some water to boil.

"Mia, would you like some hot chocolate? Mommy's going to have some tea."

"Yeah Mom."

Raphael watched from the shadows as Mia began to play with her dolls in the living room. He delivered the letter and now waited to make sure the right person found it.

The front door opened again; Mia's brother, Robbie, burst through the entryway.

"Boy, is it raining out there! Mom, coach called and said my game was cancelled. Just as well, though. I don't guess anyone feels like going anyway."

"Ok, Robbie. Would you like some hot chocolate?" Her voice revealed the grief her heart was trying to hide.

"Sure, Mom."

Robbie was right. As well done as the funeral was, it did not remove the sense of sadness, which lingered on them all.

Mary brought the hot chocolate into the living room. She sat down with her tea as they all sat in silence sipping on their mugs.

A crash of thunder, simultaneously timed with the opening of the front door, shattered the stillness. They heard footsteps coming from the entryway. Then...

"Daddy...you're home!" Mia ran to meet him and give him a hug.

Dalton hugged her back, as he reached over to give Mary a kiss and embrace.

"Sorry I'm late. I was just spending time with some of Nadia's family and friends."

"Did you see Big Mike?" Mia questioned.

"Yes I did. And he wanted you to have this...Nadia's helmet. I think it is the only thing of hers that survived the fire. Mike said she would've wanted you to have it."

"Wow...that's cool!" Robbie said. "How come Mia gets all of the cool stuff and gets to have all of the fun like being in a fire and..."

"The fire was not cool!" Dalton interrupted. "It was not great. Someone died..."

Robbie began to cry.

"Honey..." Mary said.

"I'm sorry." Dalton reached over and embraced his son. "It's just been an emotional day. And Nadia was a special lady. I knew that. But...listening to all of her firefighter friends just made me realize how incredible she was. I am still trying to figure out why I'm alive and she's not."

"Well, I am glad you're alive, honey!" Mary said with a sad smile.

"Me too, Dad." Robbie said as he hugged his father.

Mia jumped up and joined in with a tight squeeze to her dad's leg, "Me too, me too!" Mia slid down her dad's leg and then lay on the floor.

"But it is sad. I liked Nadia. She was my friend." Mia looked up at her dad, "Why did she have to die?"

"I don't know, kid. I don't know."

The entire family crawled onto the couch in one big embrace. Nobody said a word. The silence said it all.

Dalton walked through his house one more time: turning off lights and checking door locks. Mary and the kids were in bed. He stopped in the living room and picked up Nadia's helmet. It was marred with the stains of smoke and fire. Yet, he could still see the emblem on the front: "Billy's Brigade."

He sat down on the couch and held the helmet. He closed his eyes, and the events of that fateful night played out again in his mind:

"Thank you, Nadia."

"Well, don't thank me now. We're not out of here yet."

"No, I mean…thank you for saving Mia."

"Aw yeah. Sure. That's my job!"

"Well, thank you for doing it so well. I just wish my job helped people more than it does."

"Mr. Richards..."

"Please, call me Dalton."

"Ok, Dalton. You do help people with your job; you help the people you represent."

"But, I have also hurt a lot of people in the process."

"Do you think I haven't lost some people along the way, doing what I do?"

"But that's different! You at least give people a chance to live. To be honest, I am just trying to make more money."

"Do you like your job?"

"Yeah, most of the time. But not tonight."

"Well, why don't you try to take more cases and represent people that really need help?"

"Yeah...I could do that. It just doesn't pay as well!"

Dalton and Nadia both laughed.

"I was supposed to be at my son's soccer awards banquet tonight. Instead, I was trying to make more money, and I put my daughter's life in danger."

"Ok, Foxy...We're on our way back up." Big Mike's voice boomed over the radio.

"Well, Dalton, I guess we'll have to finish this conversation another time. Right now, why don't we let ourselves get rescued?"

"Sounds..."

Dalton never finished his sentence. He never had the chance to shake Nadia's hand. The last thing he saw was her smile, as the roof above and the floor below crashed in at the same time. Somehow, he ended up outside, on the ground, without a scratch on him.

He opened his eyes and stared again at Nadia's helmet. He wiped his tears and stood up. "You deserve to be in the trophy case, Miss Dumont."

He opened up a glass case filled with the kids' competitive ribbons and trophies. He began to clear out a space to put Nadia's helmet. As he moved one of his son's soccer trophies, an envelope slipped out and fell to the floor. Dalton put the helmet in its new spot and closed the glass door. As he stepped back, he heard something crinkle under his shoe. He reached down to see what it was. He picked up the envelope and saw his name.

He opened up the envelope and began to read. He quickly made his way over to the couch and sat down.

Mr. Richards, or should I say Dalton,

Are you sitting down? If you can't believe that you're reading this, I can't believe that I'm writing it! Well, someone is helping me write this letter. I guess there is no way to explain what I mean.

We did say we were going to finish our conversation at another time, didn't we? This will be a little one-sided though.

Listen, I don't know how, and I don't know why, but I have the chance to leave my final words with one person. Now, I know you may be asking, "Why me?"

To be honest, I don't have a lot of family. I was an only child and both of my parents are dead. As you know, my marriage did not make it and we never had any children. Be it good or bad, I was married to the fire department. The guys of "Billy's Brigade" were my only real family. "Why didn't I leave this letter with them?" you are probably asking. Dalton, I had to think about making the most impact with the final moment of my life on the earth. All my boys at Billy's Brigade are married to the fire department. They are going to keep doing what they do because it is who they are. Besides, I know they will dedicate their service now to me. That is a given. It is just the way they are.

But Dalton, in the brief time I spent with you and Mia, I saw something. I heard something in your voice when we talked that I had not seen when you were just being my husband's attorney. Dalton, I saw a man that is not being who he really wants to be. The world needs good attorneys, and you are one. However, is that all you want? Just to be a good attorney?

Your little Mia is something else and she needs her dad not an attorney. All little girls need their dads. My dad died when I was twenty-one. I never stopped missing him. Your little Mia sure loves you. You can see it in her eyes and in the fact that she ran into a burning building to find you.

Can you imagine if this whole scenario had turned out different? I don't know if you noticed, but some bizarre happenings took place in that fire. I have been a firefighter for long enough to have seen a lot of crazy stuff. But what went on that night was unexplainable. Smoke parting in front of us like Moses parting the Red Sea, and me even finding you and Mia. Then, that bright light shining on that room surrounded by smoke and fire—but somehow not on fire.

Next, when the whole thing crashed in, you and I were only three feet apart, and here I am and there you are. How is it possible that you even survived?

I am going to tell you something that most people do not know about me. I believe. What do I mean? I mean that...I believe in God. Well, more than believe. I talk to Him...often. I have a relationship with Him. It is because of Him that I had the courage to go into burning buildings and rescue people. It is because of Him that I was able to go on when I lost my parents.

The reason I am telling you this is that I believe what happened that night was because of God. It was... you know... supernatural. I don't know why I wasn't rescued, but I am okay with that. I trust God, and I am ready to go meet Him.

The question is...are you? I trust that you were rescued for a reason. You were given a second chance in life. He rescued you for a purpose. How else can you explain what happened? You should be dead. You know it; I know it; and all of my guys that saw the fire know it. My next question to you is...what are you going to do about it?

You have a chance to be the man you really want to be. Be it. Make your life count. Be the dad you really want to be. Be courageous in the way you live. Be an example to your kids and a best friend to your wife. If you stay an attorney, really help people.

Don't just live for yourself, and don't sacrifice your family for your job. Because honestly, losing my marriage is my only regret in life. However, don't be crying over me. Where I am going, there are no more regrets! I am going to a good place, and I am going to see Him!

Dalton, the most important thing I can leave you with is this: use your second chance to turn to God. He loves you and will help you. He will save you; He is the only one who can.

If you want to do something for me, make my sacrifice count. Take advantage of your second chance. Not many people get one.

And for the love of God, take care of that little Mia. She sure is a cutie! Give her a kiss for me, will you?

Nadia

"Daddy, are you ok?" Mia crawled up on Dalton's lap.

"What?" he was surprised to see her. "Oh, hey my little princess! What are you doing up?"

"I couldn't sleep and I saw the light on. What are you doing Daddy? Have you been crying?"

"I was just thinking."

"'Bout Nadia?"

"Yes, about Nadia."

"Why are you staring at that blank piece of paper?"

Dalton looked at the letter from Nadia. He wondered if he was the only one who could see the writing.

"Dad...what is that?" Mia pointed at the letter.

"Oh...nothing." Dalton looked at the letter again. Apparently, it was only for him. He folded it and put it in his pocket as he smiled at Mia and said, "How about we go in the kitchen and see if we can find a snack?"

"Right now? But Dad...it's late."

"Yeah, you are right. Maybe we shouldn't."

"I guess we could have just a little snack."

"That sounds good." Dalton knelt down and looked into Mia's eyes, "Mia, do you know how much your daddy loves you?" He hugged her tight.

"Daddy, I love you too. Now what are we gonna eat?"

Dalton laughed.

Mia ran into the kitchen, "C'mon, Dad...let's go."

Dalton turned and looked back toward the trophy case one more time. He then looked up, "Thank you, Nadia...thank you."

He began to walk toward the kitchen and stopped again. He looked up once more, "God, hi...it's Dalton. I think it's time we met."

CHAPTER 19

The tires screeched. The headlights dimmed. A purple bike with a white basket and flower-covered seat flew into the air—mangled, bent, empty. A little six-year-old girl lay in the road—beautiful, innocent, lifeless. A scream came from the gathering crowd...

The tires screeched. The headlights dimmed. The bike flew. The little girl lay lifeless. Somebody screamed. The tires screeched. The headlights dimmed. The bike flew. The little girl lay lifeless. Somebody screamed. The tires screeched. The headlights dimmed. The bike flew. The little girl lay lifeless. Somebody screamed...

Marilyn awoke in a panic-induced pool of sweat. The dream was back again; the same dream. Like a big screen feature that would not change. It had been playing for two months—ever since the night she watched her little girl die.

"Melany...oh my dear, sweet Melany!"

She grabbed her pillow and held it tight.

"Mommy loves you...I miss you. Please come home! Won't you please come back? I bought you a brand-new bike! And you and

Mommy can ride for hours. And I will always ride right beside you. I will never let you ride alone..."

An unstoppable wave of grief took over. Marilyn sobbed deeply as she hugged and kissed the pillow in her hands.

"Oh, Melany, I love you. Mommy will never let you out of her sight again. I promise. Just come back to Mommy. Please! Pleeease! Please come back!"

Frank, Marilyn's husband, stood out of sight in the hallway. He let out a silent sigh. He closed his eyes and dreamed of better days: days that were, days he hoped for, days that never would be again.

"Who was she?"

Marilyn startled, turned toward the unexpected voice. She reluctantly spoke, "Oh...she was my daughter; my six-year-old daughter."

She was standing in front of Melany's grave. She stood there often, sometimes for hours.

"I'm sorry." Patrice spoke with genuine concern. "I know what it's like to lose a child. Of course, not one this young. But still...too young to die."

"Excuse me...do I know you?"

"No, I don't think you do." Patrice let out a slight smile and reached out her hand. "I'm Patrice or Mrs. Lincoln if you prefer."

"Listen, I don't want to be rude, but...I really don't feel like talking right now," Marilyn said.

"I understand." Patrice now stepped closer and placed her hand on Marilyn's shoulder.

"Believe me, dear, I know the last thing you want is an old Italian woman interrupting your time with your daughter. And yes, I am Italian as I am sure you can tell by my speech. Even though my last name is not Italian, that is just because I did not marry an Italian man. Which, I might add, my mother was not too happy about. Come to think of it…neither was my father."

Marilyn stared at her speechless. She could not hide her "why are you telling me this" expression.

"Oh, what am I doing? I apologize. Here you are grieving over the worst loss of your life, and I am rambling on about nothing important. I am sorry. I just need to tell you something."

Marilyn could not fathom what this woman, that she did not even know, could possibly have to tell her. Marilyn just wanted to be alone.

With her eyebrows scrunched and mouth turned down, she looked at Patrice. "What is it you want to tell me?"

Patrice took Marilyn by the hands and held them.

She looked Marilyn right in the eyes as she spoke, "Your daughter, Melany…she is just fine. You need to know that she is being well taken care of. And she is in no pain: experiencing no sorrow."

"How can you know that? And…how do you know her name?"

"Well, dear, I know her name because it is right there on the stone: no other reason. And as far as how I know she is ok, well…you will just have to trust me on that one. This old Italian lady has a feeling. I don't know if you are religious or not, but I have gotten to know the 'man upstairs' pretty good if you know what I mean."

"You're talking about God?"

"Yes, dear one; I am talking about God."

"Well…He and I aren't talking right now. I don't think He would want to hear what I have to say. Besides…He took my little girl, and I can never forgive Him for that."

"I believe I know how you feel. Like I said, I too lost a little girl. She was older, and she and I did not always get along, but…she was still my little girl. Lucinda was her name."

"Listen, I know you are just trying to help and all, but why are you telling me this? I mean…we don't even know each other; I really just want to be left alone. Don't take it personal. You know how I feel, right?"

"OK. I will leave you alone. However, before I do, let me share a little from my heart. Believe me, deary, this old lady does not want to argue with you or cause you any more grief. As if that were even possible after what you have been through. I'll tell you what…give me five minutes just because I am old and each minute may be my last so I should be able to do what I want to with them."

Patrice smiled an irresistible old Italian momma smile that made it difficult to say "no."

Marilyn could not believe the old lady. *Is she serious?* She thought to herself, *Are you kidding me? Do I have a big sign on me that says 'All nuts and flakes welcome?' As if I am not in enough pain, I need some old lady I don't even know to share with me her senile ramblings on God and her own experiences. Please!*

Patrice patiently waited for an answer; her body language revealed no signs of going away.

Reluctantly, Marilyn responded, "Ok. But please make it quick."

"Alright, my dear; as you wish."

Still wishing to be alone, Marilyn braced herself. The old Italian lady was not giving her a choice.

Off to the side about thirty yards away, Raphael was hiding behind a tree. He watched the entire occurrence take place. He admired the persistence Patrice displayed.

Raphael was not there to deliver a letter or to complete a rescue. In fact, he was not there on official business at all. This was his day off. Raphael was there because he enjoyed checking in on people: those who had received a letter or the gift of rescue. He actually trailed Patrice to this place. This was not the first time he had followed her.

He followed many people, though he did not always like what he saw when he checked in on them. Not everyone was better. Raphael observed that no matter how much divine intervention people received in their lives, some never got over their tragedies. Sadly, some never turned to the Commander either.

Raphael loved checking in on Patrice, though. She had made peace with herself and built a wonderful relationship with the Commander. In fact, they talked all of the time. She loved Him and it showed. With the Commander's help and guidance, Patrice turned tragedy into triumph. She spent most of her time doing what she was doing right now: talking to others who experienced a great loss. She also prayed; and the Commander listened. He heard the cry of her heart for others and answered her prayers again and again. She figured out what many never do: *all things work together for the good of those who love the Commander and who answer His call to be a part of His plans.*

She still missed Lucinda. She still cried sometimes. However, the Commander healed her heart in such a way that peace now resided where heartache had reigned. She now felt the pain of others while carrying the power of hope and an inexplicable joy that only the Commander can give. She learned how much the Commander wants to heal the broken hearted; and how much He desires a relationship with everyone. Since turning to the Commander, she made it her life's mission to share His love, hope, and forgiveness with everyone she met: especially those who were grieving or without hope.

Seeing how her life changed for the better encouraged Raphael in his own assignment and mission.

Today, Raphael was not alone. As small as he was for an angel, there was a figure beside him who was even smaller: Melvin—his newly acquired intern. Raphael decided to use his day off to do a little training.

Melvin had a notepad and pen that he used to write down everything Raphael did, said, or even thought about saying. He was a nervous little angel whose eyes darted back and forth searching for something to observe.

Raphael looked down at Melvin and rolled his eyes. This new intern was testing Raphael. He would have to trust the Commander once again.

Raphael returned to training mode, "All right, Melvin. Are you getting all of this?"

"Sir, yes sir! Getting it all, sir!"

"You can stop calling me sir."

"Ok, sir. Whatever you want, sir."

Raphael let out a deep sigh. "Okay, as I was saying earlier, it is not always the outcome of a mission that makes it a success, it is being obedient. The Commander will take care of the outcome; we just do what we know to do."

"Sir, how do we know what to do?"

"You just know," Raphael said as his thoughts drifted off into a hundred different memories.

A slideshow of faces revolved through his mind. He thought about all of the people with whom he had been involved. He remembered the whole "JB incident." He thought about his conversations with Michael and even his meeting with the Commander.

"Sir, sir, you were saying...you just know?"

Raphael returned from his momentary trip down memory lane, "Oh yes, sorry, Melvin. Yeah, you just know...the Commander makes sure of that. I mean, you have this..." Raphael held up his hi-tech notebook.

Melvin stared at it with awe, "Wow…will I get one of those?" he said as he looked at his own tattered notebook.

"Well, maybe. That's not up to me."

Raphael looked back and saw Patrice holding Marilyn in her arms. He smiled.

"All right, now do you see the way she reached out to the woman who was grieving? As I said before, the outcome of a mission is not how we measure our success. However, it is always nice to see someone like Patrice. She truly understands her mission…the mission…His mission."

Raphael's voice trailed off. He was lost in his own thoughts again.

"If enough of these humans would realize how much the Commander loves them, well…there would not be a need for what we are doing." Raphael hesitated and then spoke more to himself than to Melvin, "And you know…I would be just fine with that."

"Sir, grieving? What is this grieving you speak of?" Melvin was looking up at Raphael with pen in hand ready to write something down.

Raphael breathed out another sigh as he stared at Melvin.

"Patience…I had to ask the Commander for the gift of patience," Raphael spoke under his breath.

"What was that, sir? She is a patient?" Melvin scribbled something on his notepad. "So, is this lady we are following a doctor of the grieving you spoke of?"

Raphael smiled as he shook his head. He looked down at Melvin, "You know what...that's enough training for today. How about if we pick this up again tomorrow?"

"Okay, sir. Whatever you think, sir. But I do hope we will be talking more about this doctor of grieving and the patients and why we are hiding behind this tree and when I can get a cool notebook and why we are training on a day off and what..."

Raphael flew up into the sky as he listened to Melvin's voice trail off.

"Sir? Where did you go? Uh...sir...sir?" Melvin looked up, "Oh, there you are. Wow, you are fast. Wait up, sir!"

"Please stop calling me sir!"

"Yes, sir. Whatever you say, sir."

Raphael looked down at Patrice and Marilyn as he flew away, "Keep doing what you are doing, Patrice. Keep doing what you are doing."

CHAPTER 20

Hello,

My name is Raphael. I have no last name. As far as who I am and what I do, well...

...I work for someone who knows you very well. You may or may not know Him. I know Him as the Commander. He is my boss. You would know me as an angel. He has many who work for Him, and we all have diverse assignments. Mine is not well known. However, I have learned to appreciate my assignment, and I enjoy being a part of the Commander's plan.

"Why am I telling you all of this?" Well, in my line of work, I spend most of my time collecting the words and thoughts from those who needed to say something before they left this place. Now, the Commander has given me the opportunity to leave my own UnWritten letter. He has asked that I stay within the rules that are already established: which means I can only leave this letter with one person. Therefore, I have chosen to leave it with you.

Please know that since I only have one shot at this, I am going to be very open and transparent with what I say. Please take what I have to share with you to heart.

With the time I have spent with humans on this earth, I have observed and learned many things. I have seen the best of the Commander's creation, and I have seen the worst. I have seen why the Commander loves humans and why they often break His heart. I have seen the fruit of bitterness and the lack of forgiveness. I have witnessed the benefits of kindness and compassion. I have seen humans lay down their lives for the sake of others, and I have seen humans take life away.

With all that I have observed, my advice to you is this: do not leave any UnWritten Letters in your heart. Tell people you love and appreciate them today! You may not have tomorrow. Do not waste your time on bitterness and being unforgiving. Do not wait to be kind to those around you; do not wait to give your life away for something that matters. Be quick to say you are sorry and be slow to anger. Do not argue over trivial matters. Smile as often as you can. Encourage everyone you meet. Do not be critical. Give people a chance to change. Treat others the way you want to be treated. Resolve your issues as quick as possible, because unresolved issues of today become the regrets of tomorrow. Do not try to control other people's lives, but do your best to live a life worthy of imitating. Be humble and not proud, the Commander will lift you up at the right time. Do not be jealous of what others have, be thankful for what you have no matter how insignificant it may seem. Take responsibility when you mess up. Do not blame other people for your mistakes. Learn from your mistakes and move on, rather than allowing your mistakes to rule you for the rest of your existence in this momentary realm. If you have hurt others by what you have done, be sorry for your actions and willing to make restitution.

I have seen many humans live their lives just getting through another day. I must tell you, after spending time with the Commander and hearing His heart...that is not His plan. You have the ability and opportunity to do more than exist. You have the opportunity to truly live. You have the chance to leave a powerful legacy. Your decisions can and will affect the next generation. You can make changes in your life today that will affect your children, your grandchildren, and your great grandchildren. Most humans do not realize how much influence they have. Unfortunately, when influence is not properly directed, it becomes misdirected. The result is a misguided legacy. It is important to know, whether you are trying to or not, you are leaving a legacy. You can leave a legacy of destruction, or you can leave a legacy of life.

The Commander desires for you to leave a legacy worth passing on. Many humans want to leave a heritage of what they call success. I must be honest; many people do not have the same definition of success as the Commander. They toil, sweat, and spend their days working for something that will not last. They pour all of their energy and efforts into laboring for a better life and, in the end, they are just tired, frustrated, and empty. They have spent their days in pursuit of life without realizing that life is only found when you give your life away. The Commander set the example for all of His creation in that department.

I must be honest, I do not understand everything that happens and why. However, I do know the Commander has a plan; and those that truly know Him become a part of this plan. They find purpose by becoming a part of His purpose. They realize this life is not the end. There is more: so much more.

I wish I could tell you everything I have seen and learned. However, I will not take away from the opportunity for you to find out for yourself. There is a powerful way you can do this.

Did you know the Commander wrote a letter? Many people have read His letter and do not understand what He said. I do not have time to tell you everything in the letter, but I will share with you the general theme.

The Commander is full of love. In fact, He is love. He did not need to create humans, but He wanted to. He desired to share His love. Wanting His relationship with humans to be real, He gave them the ability to choose. This meant they could choose to receive or reject His gift of love; and they could choose to have a relationship with Him or not. He left it in their hands. The humans chose to do their own thing and turned from the love of the Commander. Their relationship was lost. This broke His heart, but He never stopped loving them. The Commander longed to have the relationship with the people He created restored. He knew He would have to pay a price to purchase back the relationship that had been lost. He also knew that the price would be high. What could match the price of a life: much less, the life of billions? What is a life worth? Is a life worth a dollar? ...a million dollars? ...a billion dollars? In truth, life is priceless. The only thing that could buy His most prized creation back was another life. However, it had to be a life that was pure, unblemished by bad choices and wrong decisions. Knowing this, the Commander did something extraordinary: He sent His Son to die for all people in order to show His love for them. By sending His Son, the Commander gave His life for the life of all. He purchased back His relationship with all people. Here is the catch though...humans still have to decide to receive His love and acknowledge the price that was paid for them. Otherwise, they remain lost without the Commander.

I do not want to give away all of the best parts of the Commander's letter, because you should read it for yourself. Nevertheless, I do need to let you know one more part that is incredible. The Commander did send His Son to die for you, but...He did not stay dead! He was so full of life; He would not stay in the grave! I know this sounds a little crazy, but it is true. The Commander and His Son are waiting to meet you. Believe me, I have met the Commander and have listened to Him share His heart. I cannot put into words how much He loves you.

Do not be afraid to cry out to Him. Do not be afraid to talk to Him. Believe me; He is listening. He is always listening.

I think I will end my letter now. However, before I do, let me give you one more piece of advice: Read the Commander's letter for yourself, it will change your life now and for all eternity.

In there you will find out how to know Him. In there you will find out how to have a relationship with Him. In there you will discover how to talk to Him. In there you will find out how to live a life worth living that will never end.

Well, that is all I have. I actually have to go meet with the Commander right now. We have to discuss my new intern... Melvin. Wow, the stories I could tell you about him. Please pray for me!

Hoping to see you in another place at another time. In the mean time, go live for Him, and leave no part of your life UnWritten.

Joyfully Serving the Commander,

Raphael

H.E Hobson

Hobson has worked as a minister for over 22 years. He holds a Bachelor's degree from Roberts Wesleyan College and is a graduate of the Teen Mania Honor Academy. As well, Hobson has lead mission teams in over ten different countries.

Hobson currently serves as an assistant pastor at New Hope Worship Center in Batavia, NY, where he resides with his beautiful wife, Melissa, and four wonderful children—Haleigh, Bryce, Keatyn, and Josiah.

www.harlanhobson.com